Gumbo

Gumbo

by Mack Thomas

Grove Press, Inc.   New York

Several sections from this novel were previously pub-
lished: Magnolia, Folksong, and Revival in *Evergreen
Review;* Fig Newton, Hard-Rock Candy, and Apple in
Saturday Evening Post; Green Grapes in *Cosmopolitan.*

MANUFACTURED IN THE UNITED STATES OF AMERICA
BY THE BOOK PRESS, BRATTLEBORO, VERMONT

Contents

Magnolia

WHEN THE SKY GOT DARK and clapped its hands, Toby wrapped himself in a blanket and sat on the wooden porch that mouthed the front of the house, watching the noisy sky make blue-white cracks that healed at once without a trace of a scar. The claps of sky hands weren't hand-claps at all. Papa said the noise was an old old woman up there spilling a sack of potatoes on a

7

bridge. But to watch the wind bend the rain . . .

The ditch would hide all but its wide in a rust-red anger of water as the draining rain fled down the red clay slant of Luke Street hill. When the rain gentled to the first sign of friendliness, Toby threw the blanket aside and ran from the porch to wade in the six-inch thrill of river in the ditch. That was when he had to make his feet remember the broken glittery that bit his toes and heels and made them leak hurt.

Down the ditch and down the sand that burned when the sun was mad stood another house. He liked to play at another house. It had a hole in the ground, a hole big down beneath a top and shelves on its cool damp walls. The shelves had glitteries not gone to pieces, hollow glitteries, whole and filled with peaches and pears and good things to eat. There were other things in the glitteries, things all right to look at but not what Toby liked to eat. But Papa said things like, "Eat them turnip greens, Toby. Make you get big and put hair on your chest," so he ate them.

By the time the leaves got too dirty to keep and the trees started throwing them away, Toby knew that "work" was something Papa got at the mill. The mill was the biggest house in the world. It was white, and had four rows of windows. Everyone got "work" at the mill, all the Papas and most of the Mammas, too. One day, waiting for Papa to beat the dark to the house, Toby saw a thing in the sky, coming across the top of the mill. The color wasn't bad . . . about like the wavy sheets of tin that kept the rain from coming through the top of the house . . . but it made a noise like a busy bee caught in each ear. It came slow through the almost startime sky and looked like a Toby eater. He got too scared to notice he had pulled an arm off Celia's pickaninny doll. It came straight at him and was going to get him but went on overhead. Able to move again because the big thing hadn't seen him and wasn't going to swallow him, Toby dropped the doll and the arm and scuttled around the corner of the house, wanting to keep it in sight at least until the noise got out of his ears. The trees were about to be in the way. He thought of the cellar mound and started for the house next door. Then someone was crying in the back yard. Listening made it Celia's. He ran to her without another thought about the thing that hunted in the sky.

Rounding the corner, he saw her standing by the back steps, holding the doll and the loose arm to herself and trying to stop crying. He went to her, wanting to hug her leg or pull her skirt or something. The door opened and Mamma stepped out on the small wooden porch at the top of the wooden steps. Mamma looked at Celia and doll and arm and Toby, stepped back in the kitchen for a few seconds, then came out and down the three steps, the stinging stick in her hand.

Celia watched her come with the sting-Toby-look in her eyes. She dropped one hand to a fold and hid Toby in the swirl of her skirt, and said, "Don't whip him, Mamma. He didn't mean to do it."

Mamma stood still, looking at Celia with eyes full of stars and softness. "You're a good child, Celia," she said. Then she took Celia by the hand and reached into Celia's skirt and found Toby. He knew by the way her arm felt on his elbow that it was all right to come out. She aimed all of their eyes with her own, aimed them at the mill. After a bit she said, "We'd better get on in the house. It's getting dark."

Not long after the cold came, Papa stopped leaving every morning. There seemed to be lots of Papas around, and the mill noise had died. Papa didn't smell like work anymore. He walked to the mill every day and stood by the little white house at the mill gate, talking with the other Papas and looking up into the naked branches of the cottonwood trees. He took Toby with him now and then. The Papas stood around making marks on the ground with the blunt toes of their shoes, talking in low voices, not laughing too often or for very long when they did. Gathering the crisp brown leaves into playing piles, Toby looked up from time to time and found Papa watching him with a hurt in his eyes.

Papa left the house one morning and didn't come home till startime. He came through the door so happy the screen slammed. Toby got grabbed up and thrown into up there, too fast for his breath to go with him. It was good, and he was glad. Papa hadn't done him in a long time. Sometimes, if Papa's face looked right and words had singing in them, a run and a hug of his leg and a beg of "Do me! Do me!" made him grab and throw Toby almost to the top of up there in the house.

But not in a long time. Lately, begs made Papa put the heavy in his hand on Toby's head as he said, "You go along now, Toby."

Mamma came, giving the wet of her hands to her apron, taking Papa with, "Gracious! What's all this commotion?"

Toby's feet came down to the floor, then Papa's hands went out to Mamma. "Work!" said Papa. "Katherine, I got work!"

Mamma made wet eyes. Toby tried to make himself another throw from Papa. Mamma's wet eyes made it hard to think about, but wanting it took him to Papa, pulling at his trousers, begging, "Do me do me do me!"

Mamma wouldn't let him play under the house anymore. "You'll take cold and die," she said. Since the sun stopped getting mad, the air made hurt in his chest when he stayed outside too long. Maybe that made the new smell for Papa's work. It wasn't like the other. Maybe the new work Papa had was taking cold and die. Wondering about getting work and the new work smell and the hurt of breathing the air outside made a change in the way it felt to think about Papa.

Celia said Christmas was coming. Jenny tried to tell about Santy Claws, but Celia had to do it to make it real. Papa came home in the bright one day and sat at the table with Mamma so they could pass a new sad back and forth with their eyes.

Celia went every day to learn about wigglies, and there was a worry. The smell of work was gone, even the new one that dirtied knees and smelled like under the house. Papa got the asking with Celia away. "What you troubling yourself about work for, Toby?" Papa answered. "You'll learn about it, soon enough." The way he said it made Toby think it was good and bad, all at once.

A man brought a flat little sack with a picture and wigglies on the front. In the dark that night, Toby listened to Mamma and Papa talk about it. Papa said, "It's not that I want to go, Katherine, but I've got to. There's things we need, and Christmas has to come or I can't look myself in the face."

Mamma said, "Mississippi . . . it's such a long way. Something's bound to turn up soon. The mill might start up any day."

"Now Kate," said Papa, "You know that ain't so."

"Winter setting in so hard and all," said Mamma. "And with Christmas . . . I hate to have you gone."

"Don't make it harder, Kate," said Papa. "I got to go. That's maybe the only mill in the country still running. If it wasn't for Albert Jennings . . . well . . . we ought to be thankful."

"I know," said Mamma, "but . . . well . . . have you figgered a way to get there? Traveling needs money, and you know . . ."

"I'll get there," said Papa. "Never you mind about that. There's freight trains every day, going all the way to Biloxi."

Toby fell asleep wondering what a freight train

might be. Papa was gone next morning. At breakfast, Jenny asked, "Mamma, where's Papa?" Before Mamma could say anything, Toby said, "Gone to Luxi ona fray-train!"

The man who brought the flat little sack with a picture and wigglies came with another one a few days later. This one had something in it that Mamma called "money."

Christmas came. Lights on trees seemed a good thing to Toby. He couldn't stay awake and missed seeing Santy Claws, but liked the smooth round colored glitteries and the feathers that went around his head like the ones in Celia's book with the picture that showed what Indians wear.

Between every church day the man came with a new letter, as Mamma called it, and money.

The bad of winter came, and the only outside Toby got was to the toilet. Celia came home every day with words that she read from her books for Toby. Sometimes, even while she read, he got something in his head about something gone, something he wanted but couldn't remember, and sometimes the gone and the wanting made him cry.

The only play from Jenny got to be letting her wrap him with rags. Baby learned to walk, but not very far.

One day Toby went outside to the toilet and ran back in the house with a shout. "The sun's gettin' mad again, mad again, mad again!" It wasn't long before the trees started speckling themselves with new leaves.

Orby's Papa came to see Mamma. "Write Tobias," he said. "The mill is startin' up again next week." After he left, Mamma sat at the table and cried. Toby waited all he could, then asked, "What'sa matter?"

Mamma said, "Your Papa's coming home." Toby tried to think of what Papa looked like but couldn't remember.

Mamma mailed a letter. A sitting down to eat supper came that had the door flying open and a man coming into the kitchen. Toby looked at him and remembered. Everyone got up and ran to Papa. Not Baby Pud, though. Pud sat in his highchair and started to cry. But he didn't know so it was all right.

Long after sleepy that night, long after Pud was put to bed, Papa took a paper out of a sack of things and unwrapped a twig with two shiny leaves and a flower not dirty but starting to look like the kind a tree might want to throw away. A new smell filled the room, a sweet smell, sweeter than Celia's and Mamma's hair.

Mamma said, "Now, what in the world?"

"It's a blossom of magnolia," said Papa. "All the way from Biloxi."

Mamma took it and put it to her face. After her eyes had been closed for a while, she said, "Tobias . . ."

Papa got up and went to her chair. His hand came up slow and settled on her head.

Toby watched, blinking as hard as he could to

keep his eyes from closing. He left the floor by Papa's chair and went to Papa's leg. When he wrapped his arms around it, Papa looked down. "Do me?" said Toby, knuckling the sleep in his eyes.

Dream

... THE HOUSE WAS A big square box. The four square rooms were made by the walls that crossed at the center of the box. The doors room to room were near the center, where the walls crossed, four doors, open. All four rooms were filled with people. None of their faces had names, and all were giants. Their ankles and legs were round as the trunks of trees, and the whole box trembled.

It began to move, a solid mass of feet and ankles and legs that turned counterclockwise through the rooms, a wheel of meat rotating on an axle. He tried to push out but the calves of their legs wouldn't yield to his shoulders and pressed him deeper into the corners at the center of the box. He struggled from a corner and squeezed through the door. It pressed him deeper into the next corner. With each turn through the rooms the legs and ankles and feet got closer, pressing him harder and deeper against the center and into its jawing corners. He began to scream.

The pace remained the same. The legs, the feet, the ankles moved closer. The pressure became hard and steady. He couldn't breathe, and it seemed that things were beginning to burst inside him somewhere. The pressing and bursting funneled itself up his throat and made the gush of life a breath for screaming.

The kerosene lamp on the kitchen round table turned the white oilcloth into the glittery yellow pupil of a monstrous eye. But Celia and Jenny jeweled the bedroom door with long flannel nightgowns and sleep-tangled hair falling in bands down their faces as they stared with startled mouths and wondering eyes.

There was another scream, one of annoyance. He jerked his head and snapped his eyes to Mamma standing at the kitchen sink with Pud making loud complaints in her arms.

His mouth was thick with the taste of soda dissolved in a glass of water and forced down his throat, and a quiet, almost steady voice near his ear kept saying, "It's all right, Toby. Toby? Do you hear me, son? It was just a dream . . . it's over, it's all right, son."

His Papa's arms were strong and his chest was solid and warm, and the giants were gone from the house, but not from his mind. Between his screams the glass came to his lips and the taste and the fume of soda filled his nose and choked him. His Papa went on pacing, saying, "It's all right, Toby. It's just a dream" . . . until the giants vanished from his mind as well, then he stopped screaming.

In bed with Pud asleep beside him and the house noisy and dark again, Mamma, in the other bed three feet away, said, "Oh! God have mercy! Tobias, what are we going to do . . . ?"

Papa said, "There now, Kate. I tell you, he's getting better. Why, he'll be grown right out of it by the time he's five, you wait and see."

Green Grapes

A FILM OF SWEAT caught the glare of mid-afternoon
and silvered the movements of Toby's face as he
awoke. He came from sleep uncertainly, as if five
years was not enough to get used to the strangeness
of existing. Behind their lids, his eyes called his hands
and they fisted and came up knuckling. Some of the
sweat from the slants of his nose got knuckled into the
corners of his eyes. A sting built. It was an ant, but
it wouldn't brush away like an ant. He got scared and

21

pressed his knuckles hard into his eyes. The pressing made a new thing happen in his eyes, a thing like a new way of seeing. He forgot the sting and it went away as he pressed his eyes and made skystreaks and sunsets and mountains of exploding light. When he was sure of them, he decided to save them for night when other lights aren't allowed.

The first chore he gave his eyes was to look for Pud and to see if he'd crawled from the pallet and fallen off the porch as he had the day before. He was there on the pallet but wiggled and twisted upside down from the way the nap had started. Toby looked at him close, thinking there must be some way to make him seem real. Round and fat and his thumb in his mouth . . . he didn't know you could make lights in your eyes. Baby Brother. Pud. Mamma said he was three years old.

Toby rolled his head to the other cheek and watched the heat demons dance on the red clay dust of Luke Street. After a minute or two he turned back to Pud, still wondering what "brother" meant. A thought made him climb to his hands and knees and stare straight down into Pud's face. It was easier to believe him when he was awake, shrieking and howling and wobbling around, it was easier to believe he was real. Toby decided to find out if anything moved around inside him. He put his ear on Pud's forehead, then closed his eyes and held his breath to listen good, but couldn't hear a thing. Wup! What was that? Something going "Baby, baby, baby, baby," saying it like a hump and two bumps. But what did that mean? He lifted his ear and regarded Pud with solemn concern as he tried to have other ideas for finding out if he was real.

Pud faced a different grip on the thumb in his mouth. That helped some, but it was the same thing after a minute as Pud kept sleeping hard as ever.

Toby raised himself to his knees and sat on his feet. He thought about crawling on top of Pud and rolling him across the pallet a few times. It might not prove he was real but it ought to get some kind of noise out of him and make him seem. But Pud was liable to wake up screaming, then Ceil would come running out on the porch to see what it was all about and she might even bring the switch. But even so . . .

He heard a good sound, just as he was about to sprawl across him, a sound like the kind Mr. Cuna'ham made when he was doing something at his worktable under the big tree in his back yard next door. Toby turned on the pallet and sighted down the porch into the long drapes of grapevine growing in the fenced plot that gapped the two houses. As always the sight of the guardian stout leaves on the vines reminded him to think that it ought to be cool in a place as dark green as those few grapevine rows.

He brought his eyes back to the porch and put them on the front screened door. Hard listening told him Celia was in the front room in the squeaky rocker

humming the way she did when she was doing something like stringing and snapping the green beans that
had to be put on the stove pretty soon if they were
going to be done in time for supper. With her tied up
like that she wouldn't be looking for him, not right
away, so he got on his stomach and smoothed his way
to the edge of the wooden porch. He slipped his legs
around right and then he pushed them off the edge of
the porch and raised his chest from the planks and
tilted his way to the ground with the seesaw of his hips.
And let's see Pud do that! There was no way in the
world for Pud to do that because Pud wasn't five but
three and it wasn't hard to remember what that was
like.

He crouched by the edge of the porch and looked
at Pud just long enough to make sure he wouldn't
wake up and yell. Then he almost heeled his bottom as
he kangarooed across the dry grass to Mr. Cuna'ham's
fence around the grapes.

The fence was made of big mesh wire with places
for hands and feet and not just easy but fun to climb,
so it sagged a lot. At the top Toby straddled the bend
of wire between the favorite posts that held it, and
paused to look back at the porch for a final check on
the door and on Pud. With both eyes keen on the door
he lifted the other leg over the top of the sag and
started dripping himself down the other side, ready to
jump or come back over or disappear in a puff of hope

if the front door should open. Bare foot on warm dirt whirled him from the naked fence and shuttled him under the leaves.

Wire, crosses of hickory posts and summers and winters and springs had made each row in the tiny vineyard a tunnel of leaves. The tunnels were veins where magic flowed its secret and wonderful things. The leaves caught the sunlight and sifted its scorch to a praying-mantis green that the eager green grapes would learn to love in a ripening week or two. As if that wasn't enough, there were other wonders too. Acrobat careful spiders did circus tricks on an old trapeze or two they were dangling and restringing. The hog kind of frogs that made warts on your hands if you touched them sat on themselves in the darkest spots, fanning themselves with their throats while they blinked and dozed the heat of the day away, and no matter what Celia said about moles it was a marvel to watch the seams of earth hump up and move along as the mole pawed and shouldered itself a private road ten inches under the ground.

Toby moved slowly from wonder to wonder and through the sides of the rows. Midway across the tiny vineyard he thought to listen again. He tuned in during a pause and thought for a moment he'd marveled too much on his trip through the tunnels but then the right sound started again and tickled his freckles into a smile. He reached for the drape to part himself a

portal and saw a small and round and familiar bug
make a rest stop on one of the leaves. As his hands
eased down his face sneaked close enough to study the
peppering on the lavender-orange back of the shoe-
button bug. "Ladybug, Ladybug," he chanted in a
whisper, "Ladybug, Ladybug, fly away home . . . your
house is on fire and your children are alone." The
Ladybug bared its tiny wings and maybe flew home.

He remembered again what he was in the first
place there for, and would have been pretty worried except the noise was there waiting for him to
notice it again. He arrowed quick through the tunnels
and peeped through the last wall of layered leaves.
There he was, Mr. Cuna'ham, a short round man with
hair as black as his eyes, standing solid at the end of a
solid wooden worktable, cranking a handle that turned
a wheel that made blades of hoes and knives sharp
again. The man was forty or fifty but anyhow too many
years old to actually think about and there were gold
and round rimmed glasses with tape on the parts that
hooked on his ears. A big mole on one side of his chin
had two stiff wires of white hair. There was a bend in
his arms and shoulders that said he had a wife in the
house and her name was Miz Hettie. She stayed in the
house a lot and they didn't have any kids. She called
him "Word," but his real name was Pleasant Word
Cunningham and he was principal and seventh-grade
teacher at Cottonmill School whose real name was

Samuel Pepys Elementary School or at least that's
what it said up over the schoolhouse door. Papa said
Mr. Cuna'ham had more sense than the rest of the
teachers all put together.

Mr. Cuna'ham could take his yardmower apart
and put it back together again and it would work. He
could fix clocks and make whistles out of acorns and
build birdhouses and make rubberguns and carve pro-
pellers that turned in the wind and one time made a
shoe box fly like a kite. But the best thing was that he
liked to tell things, like what made the kite stay up in
the first place and even why part of the year was so hot
it hurt to go barefooted and part of it just right and
the rest so something or other it wasn't fit for anything.

Toby saw that it would be a good day for talking.
Mr. Cuna'ham's shirt was wet and when that happened
he liked to put his hand inside his shirt and scratch.
There was no way of knowing how it worked but the
talking was better when there was scratching.

Mr. Cuna'ham stopped the wheel and the sparks
stopped flying from the knife he was sharpening. Toby
gave the vines a good shake then peeped again to see
what Mr. Cuna'ham was going to do about it. Mr.
Cuna'ham ran his thumb along the edge of the knife
and squinted and measured with his eyes and then
went back to cranking and sharpening. That was bad
because the vines might break or some leaves anyhow
if they got shook too hard. That left nothing to do but

get out in plain sight. A bunch of green grapes happened to be in a good place and Toby backed through the leaves and leaned on the vines to reach them.

The wheel stopped all at once and Mr. Cuna'-ham's big fat voice said, "What! Tearing down my grapevines? Stealing my grapes in broad daylight and . . . Oh no! Don't try to hide now Toby Siler! You're caught red-handed so come on out of there . . . that's it, come on over here. Well you ought to look guilty, I don't blame you, tearing my vines and stealing . . . didn't I tell you what to expect if you eat green grapes? And the fence! now what about the fence? I guess you've got it flat on the ground. Well, talk . . . what about it? You ought to have something to say for yourself."

Toby's big toe marked pieces of moons in the packed dirt around the table. Mr. Cuna'ham acted like the blade of the knife was the thing to look at. "And what," he said, "am I going to tell your Mamma and Papa when they come in some night and find you all doubled up from stuffing yourself with green grapes?" His glasses came around and funneled a make-believe look of concern to Toby's face. "It might be best," he said, "for you to get out the nail keg and crawl up and sit while I go in the house and try to decide what we're going to do with you."

He was quiet while Toby grunted the nail keg from under the table and near the wheel with the crank before levering himself to a seat on top. "You won't run off like a scared chicken while I'm in the house?" he asked. "No sir," Toby answered, and put one hand on the crank that turned the wheel.

Mr. Cunningham slipped the knife in his pocket and walked to the house. He stopped at the back door and looked back over his shoulder, then went inside.

When the back screen slammed in place Toby had an argument with himself about whether to stay or take off in the grapevines and home. There were one or two reasons for guessing what Mr. Cuna'ham meant to do but you couldn't be sure about grownups, not even Mamma and Papa. You could be sure of some things with Mamma and Papa but a lot of things you didn't know what to think. The wheel didn't look like it would be so hard to turn. Maybe both hands . . . Mr. Cuna'ham sure was staying gone a long time. The door-spring squeak made a fast look and then more fooling with the crank so Mr. Cuna'ham wouldn't know the things in his hands had been looked at.

Mr. Cunningham brought his serious look and the rest to the table under the tree and started setting the pair of jelly glasses and the pitcher of lemonade on the weathered boards. Filling the glasses and untying the napkins to get at the oatmeal cookies, he made his voice rough as he said, "Now Toby, you'll have to eat three or four cookies at least and drink enough of this lemonade to make them pack down around all those green grapes about to make trouble there in your stomach. I hope we're getting to it in time, that's all."

Toby would have told that he hadn't eaten a one of the green grapes that day but the oatmeal cookie tasted too good to keep thinking about that. Mr. Cunningham put one hip on the edge of the old worktable and took a big swallow from his glass before he put it on the table. He took out his handkerchief and wiped the sweat from his neck then took off his glasses and wiped behind his ears and where the red marks dented the pinch of his nose. The glasses went back in place and the handkerchief got poked into a wad in his back pocket. He took another swig of lemonade and rolled it around in his mouth and leaned back to stare up into the branches of the tree while he swallowed it.

Toby got a big chunk of cookie in his mouth and made it soft with lemonade and swallowed it whole. Mr. Cuna'ham slid his right hand past buttons and inside his shirt and Toby bit off another chunk of oatmeal cookie. Mr. Cuna'ham started scratching. "Toby," he said, "you remember that bird nest, don't you? . . . the one in the plum tree last week with the three baby birds?" He looked down from the tree and saw memory light Toby's face. "Well," he continued, "you wouldn't do anything that might hurt those baby birds, would you?"

The idea made Toby's eyes get round and big. "No *sir*, Mr. Cuna'ham," he said, swallowing hard.

"No, of course you wouldn't," said Mr. Cunningham. He took his hand from his shirt to drink from the sweaty glass, then pushed between the buttons again and scratched with a pattern that made his knuckles raise circles there inside the front of his shirt. "You see, Toby," he stalled, searching for words, "growing things . . . living things, that is, are making a trip . . . going somewhere, on their way from what they are to what they can be. No, now, there ought to be a better way of saying that, a way that makes . . . There! Look on that fence post, there where I'm pointing . . . you see that big mockingbird sitting pretty and sure of itself up on that fence post?"

"I see it!" Toby yelled. "There he goes! Going to the peach tree now!"

"Don't try to swallow when you're talking, Toby," said Mr. Cunningham. "Especially not cookies . . . you're liable to choke on a thing like that . . . but that mockingbird, now. See how big he is, compared with those babies we looked at? See how easy he made it to the peach tree? Well, those baby birds, that's where they're going . . . getting big and pretty and able to fly like that. We'll look out before long and see those baby birds all grown up and perching on fence posts unless something stops them. We've got to help growing things if we can, you and me, help them get where they are going and not do anything that might stop them or make it harder than it has to be. The growing, I mean. Like those green grapes out there, trying to get big and soft and full of good juice instead of staying little and hard and green like they are now. We've got no right to stop a thing like that from happening, now have we?"

"I wasn't trying to hurt the grapes, honest!" Toby replied.

"Ah, Toby," said Mr. Cunningham, a big grin on his round face, "I know you can't believe this but I was a boy once, just like you are now, so I know one or two of your tricks. But to get back to the grapes, it's not just them or birds I'm talking about. I want you to know it's kittens and peaches, and every growing thing in the world. People, it's about people, most of all."

Toby's thoughts took his gaze to Mr. Cuna'ham and then beyond him to the strange things without answers like leafy limbs against the sky and pictures in his own head, pictures that started into themselves and became feelings of questions with things hard to taste in their mouths. "About Pud?" he asked, something making the question come out of a place that opened and closed quicker than a surprise.

Mr. Cunningham looked happy as he said, "It's most especially about Pud, and about you, too."

Toby stood up on the nail keg, asking, "Is that what brother means?"

"Well, wait a minute, now!" said Mr. Cunningham, scratching hard. "Yes by golly! That's just what it means."

"And growing to be like Papa is going somewhere and Pud's going too?" said Toby. "And me?"

"You'll make it, too, with a little help, both of you," said Mr. Cunningham.

"Boy!" said Toby, "Wait'll Pud hears that!"

"Here," said Mr. Cunningham, his face a big round smile, "let's pour up the rest of this lemonade. Watch that ice, now, and don't swallow so fast or you'll give yourself a headache."

Toby lowered his glass and looked at the grindstone. When his breath recovered from drinking, he asked, "Can I make sparks, Mr. Cuna'ham?"

"I don't see why not," said Mr. Cunningham. He took his hip from the table and went toward the garage. He came out of the garage carrying a blunt scrap of metal. "Here," he said, handing it to Toby. "Now hold that against the wheel and I'll turn the crank. Hold it right about there so the sparks won't get in your eyes and don't fall off that keg."

Something stirred itself in Toby's memory and then was still again. He held the metal against the wheel and Mr. Cuna'ham turned the crank. It made no sparks and he took his disappointment from the wheel to Mr. Cuna'ham's face. "You're not holding it hard enough," said Mr. Cunningham. "You've got to press hard."

The thing Toby had almost remembered jumped up and down in his mind. He pressed the metal against the wheel and laughed at the layer of sparks that appeared. Mr. Cunningham turned the wheel faster while he grinned.

"Tobeee," someone called from across the tiny vineyard. "Tobee Si-lerrr. You better answer me!"

Mr. Cunningham stopped the wheel, and said, "That sounds like Celia wanting you home. You'd better scoot."

Toby jumped from the keg, feet ready for running. "Wait!" said Mr. Cunningham. "Put this last cookie in your pocket and take it to Pud. And don't forget what we talked about!"

Toby slipped the cookie in his pocket and took off around the house toward Luke Street, calling, "Bye, Mr. Cuna'ham."

Celia was on the front porch with her hands on her hips when he came round the vineyard. Pud was awake and naked on the pallet. His wet short pants were there in a pile on the porch, a clean pair close by. Like always, his face was red from the crying that waking up made him do. He started crying again when he looked and saw Toby. Celia said, "Now just where have you been? I ought to switch you good, Toby Siler, running off that way and leaving Pud here on this porch by himself!"

"I didn't run off, honest, Ceil," said Toby. "Mr. Cuna'ham was telling me something."

"Come on up here and put those clean pants on him!" said Celia. "And you'd better stay right here

and watch him. There's supper to fix and I can't be
screaming and chasing after you." She turned toward
the door and opened it, but before she went into the
house she looked back and added, "I mean it now,
don't you run off again!"

She went inside and Toby dropped to the pallet.
He started working the pants over Pud's bare feet and
up his legs. Pud found a breath he didn't need for
screaming and used it to blurt, "You hide! Hide from
Pud!" then started screaming again.

"Aww Pud, I didn't hide from you," said Toby.
He got the pants on Pud's legs and got Pud on his
hands and knees so the pants would come up on his
hips. "Here, look!" he said, sending one hand on a
round trip to his pocket. "See!" he said, "I brought you
a cookie! Stand up so it can button."

Pud got up and took the cookie while his pants
fell down around his feet. It took pulling and tugging
to get them over his hips again and buttoned in place.
Pud was down to the last bite of cookie by then. When
that was gone he got his face all stretched out of shape
and open-mouthed again. "'You run off and hide!" he
bawled.

Toby put both of his arms around Pud, saying,
"You're my *brother*, Pud! Don't cry and I'll tell a
secret!"

Pud sniffed and gave Toby a wet doubtful look. "A
s-s-secrit?" he stuttered.

"I can make sparks in my eyes!" said Toby. He

closed his hands and raised a curve of knuckles to each of his eyes. "Like this," he said. "Do it hard."

Pud watched for another second or two before he dropped to the porch with a thump of his bottom and started crying again.

School

MISS HELEN BELL taught the only First grade at Cotton-mill School. It was quite a thing for Miss Bell, her being a thinking woman, and for Toby, too, that first day when Mamma brought him to school. She had a little advance information, of course. She was a sort of outsider, not quite, but still, but anyhow she lived at the edge of Cottonmill and it's hard to tell if she was facing out or in. But anyhow she had advance information on Young Master Toby Siler, as she got a kick out of calling him in her thoughts. During the years when he was between the ages of three and six she'd just in the natural course of things had a chance to look him over when she ran into him at Trager's Store. She was first attracted the day she noticed the expressions he wore when he looked at things. Too, she thought there was something free in the way he walked, something that might always be absolutely effortless. She wanted to know more but believed in letting things happen in their own good time.

The first day he came to school she touched the strong hand that she held against the faucet of the drinking fountain to show him how it worked. The second day she saw the serviceable blue eyes look at every picture in the reader as he turned the pages, one by one. She knew by then that he knew how to read, but still she was concerned about his interest in pictures.

The third day she asked him to wait after school. When the rest of the children were gone she called him to her desk, and said, "Do you see this little stool here under my desk?—just let me get it out—yes—this is for you."

Toby climbed to the top of the stool with almost no trouble at all. As he was settling himself, Miss Bell said, "It will be just right before the year is over and after you've grown a bit."

"I know what growing means," said Toby. "Growing is going somewhere."

"Why, yes," said Miss Bell, "That's very good." She straightened something on her desk while she smiled at something in her head, then she palmed her palms and her forearms together and aimed them down her slender lap straight into his open heart. "Toby," she said, on the edge of a secret, "do you know who you are?"

"Yessum," he nodded, wide-eyed, "I'm Toby Siler."

"Oh, please forgive me, Toby," she said. "That *isn't* a very good question, is it? But let me ask a better one: tell me, do you know *what* you are?"

"Yessum," Toby grinned and swung his feet, "I'm a boy!"

"Well, all right," she said, a look on her face that she was thinking. "Now," she said, her eyes getting bright, "let's pretend we can say anything."

Toby gave her a wondering look that slowly became a new idea. "Ohhh," he said, "you mean anything at all?"

"Yes!" she said, her face happy. "That's just what I mean! Now, tell me what you are."

After a moment the smile got off Toby's face so it could look suspicious and a little afraid. "I can't," he said, and dropped his eyes to his feet hanging still just off the floor.

"Of course you can," said Miss Bell. "You can tell me."

He raised his eyes at last and looked at her face. "You got to tell it first," he said.

"All right," she nodded, and looked over his head in a way that made him think she was leaving. "I'm a leaf on a tree," she said, "and the wind is blowing. I'm a sky that wants to make a rainbow, just waiting for the first warm rain."

"I'm a bird that flies after supper at night," said Toby eagerly.

"Yes!" said Miss Bell, "I know the kind; fast and dark, and shaped like the edge of a saucer."

"Yeah," said Toby, caught up in it, "and looking for gnats!"

"I'm a flame the wind wants to break from its candle," said Miss Bell, a faraway look coming into her eyes.

"I'm a mangy old cat!" said Toby. "I'm a water bucket, going up and down in the well. I'm a fat old toad frog under the grapevines, going 'Blink! Blink!' and I'm even a giant squeezing sticky stuff out of trees, and nobody sees me!"

"Stop it!" Miss Bell cried suddenly, her hands unpalming and covering her face. "Stop it! Stop it!"

Toby half fell off the stool and stumbled backward, step by step, ignorant-minus-one as the day he was born, stammering ,"I'm Toby S-Siler . . . and . . . and . . . I'm a boy!"

Gumbo

A softness came into Miss Bell's eyes as one of her hands came away from them and started toward his face. But before touch could heal or sunder she jumped from her straight backed chair and ran to stare famish-eyed through the schoolroom windows. Toby turned and ran from the room and the building and all the way home.

From then on she liked him of course and patted his cheek and said such things as, "Oh my! Toby! That's such a pretty, bright, orange rose!"

And that was that.

Fig Newton

THE CHICKENS WERE CLIMBING each other trying to change worlds, stacking up in the corners of the chicken yard, their feet pushing and their necks pulling, their eyes about to blink out of their fool heads from the strain of trying to figure out what was going on. Pud was jumping up and down in the middle of the chicken yard, chopping the air with his arms, his feet hammering dirt the chickens had raked so fine it almost squirted as it came through his toes and out of his arches. Pud was five years old and just fat enough to jiggle a little where he lapped out around the hip hole of his farmer overalls, galluses pale across the sunburn lacing freckles thick as wild flowers on a hill all over his naked shoulders.

He turned quick as the change in his mind and made a dash for the gate. The way he yelled "Shooo!" and struggled with the gate made the chickens as scared as he was and sent them trying to go in directions that were impossible. A few out of control came straight ahead but before they could make it Pud got the gate closed somehow. He stood safe outside the chicken yard with his hands hanging in the wire on the gate and blinked back at the chickens until a look at Ceil got to be the most important thing in the world.

The September Bermuda grass around the back porch bristled the feel of the chicken yard off his feet and had them ready for the hard planks of the porch. The house was quiet behind the door screen and the kitchen looked cool and dark. Pud put his face into its sag in the screen and cupped his hands at the sides of his eyes to keep the light out and let him see inside. It looked like Mamma, her red hair hanging like a long tail of light down her shoulders, standing at the Roper stove pouring water out of a cup into the pot of beans. Mamma and Papa hadn't come in from work yet and the wave of feeling broke into spray against another need, his lips moving against the screen because of the way it felt, the gurgle of the water making him say, "I'm thirsty, Ceil."

Celia put the blue lid back on the enamel pot, then came to the cabinet and dipped the cup into the water bucket. She brought it to the door, saying, "I guess you think I didn't hear you out there, scaring the living daylights out of the chickens! Get back out of the way now so the door can open." Pud stepped back, the door nudging him. Celia put her left hand high on the back of his neck and tried to put the cup to his mouth, but he started having a fit, "Me! Me!" so she let him take it and dropped her hands to her hips. He turned it up and poured water down the bib of his overalls. Celia said, "There now, do you see?" Pud opened his eyes and squinted along the cup barrel to look at her face. She tried to do something about the grin, but Pud saw it anyhow and went on drinking without missing a beat of his gulping until the cup was empty. He cradled the cup against the dribbled bib of his overalls and started gasping, "Is it . . . Ceil?" all out of breath from the drinking, "is it school-out time?"

Celia took the cup before he could break it and said, "He'll be along soon now."

Pud smeared chicken-yard dirt down his cheek and across his chin wiping the water off his face with the back of his dirty hand. His face got solemn and he said, "Chickens are crazy, ain't they Ceil?" Before she could answer he whipped off the porch and around the corner of the house, flapping his arms and shouting, "Shoo! Shoo! Shoo!"—the real chickens back in the chicken yard stiff-necked and cackling trying to decide if the commotion along the side of the house meant danger. Then Pud turned the corner at the front, and they went back to their raking.

Celia gazed off the porch, taking in the well with the bleached rope hanging dry from the pulley except down close to the bucket hung among the coils on the peg. The well door was closed good and safe, so she let her eyes move on to the thirty-seven chickens, some red and some muckled but most of them white, kind of pretty with their tomato-red combs and wattles and their legs yellow as butter. Her gaze went on through the chicken yard across the path that went through the weeds where the back yard ended, on past the Gannaway house by the railroad track, on up and along the sprawling flat line where the top of the mill slashed four floors out of the clean blue sky. The steady rustle of the mill was loud in her ears for a few seconds but faded again as she looked down the white face and the four layers of windows to the dirty cup in her hand.

She closed the door screen and brought the cup to the dishpan sitting by the water bucket on the cabinet. She frowned at the cup but couldn't get upset about it and smiled because of something that had to do with being fifteen and the oldest. One last Shoo! at the front of the house made her tilt the smile as she listened. The listening brought her head around and put the kitchen stove back in her gaze and in her mind. She started wondering if the red beans had enough salt. She went to the stove and took the stirring spoon from the top of the tall oven while her other hand closed on the butterfly potholder she'd made last year in Homemaking Class at the High School in Town. The potholder hand took the lid off the pot and the spoon hand dipped up a sample of juice. She blew on it first, but it scorched her tongue all the same when she sipped it, burnt for nothing, the beans salty enough already. The lid clanged when she clapped it back on the boiling pot. She put the spoon and the pot- holder back on the oven and turned to give the cabinet a thoughtful look as she drew her tongue across the straight edge of her upper teeth. She saw the jar of sour pickles on the second shelf and took it down. The cap and ring came off the Mason jar all right, and her lean fingers had no trouble going down the jar's throat but the pickle didn't want to be held. She decided it would be better to use a fork but ignored all that and poked and eased until she got it. She took a bite off one end and let it rest on her tongue to draw out the scorch.

The twist on the end of a cellophane bag down on the first shelf caught her eye as she put back the jar of pickles. She reached down the twist and gave the bag a feel, then took it out and saw that the Fig Newtons were down to four, and it still three days until payday. Her tongue turned the bite of pickle over while the Fig Newtons put things in her mind . . . Papa in his living-room chair with some book he was reading, fighting Indians or rivers or mountains or whatever it was right along with the rest of the people in the story, a bag of Fig Newtons in his lap . . . Toby and Pud doing something on the floor, Jenny on the edge of the sofa with her eyes glistening, watching Mamma embroider flowers on the new school blouse she'd made for her that evening . . . the cellophane crackling in Papa's lap . . . Mamma saying, "I swear I never saw a man so crazy for Fig Newtons!" . . . Papa raising his eyes and them looking at each other and grinning. . . .

Her tongue felt about as good as the scorch would let it. She chewed up the pickle and swallowed it, wondering how long it would be until Mamma could quit work and she could go back to High School. She wished 1932 was over.

The old wall clock in the living room struck four but she was sighing anyway. She put the Fig Newtons back on the shelf. Her pecan eyes got serious and she looked down in the meal bin to see if there was going to be enough for the supper cornbread. That was all right, so she took a pan of potatoes and a paring knife to the kitchen table and sat in one of the dark-oak kitchen chairs and started the peeling.

Straddling the big tin breadloaf mailbox up on the hickory post at the front of the yard, Pud saw Jenny and Toby coming up Luke Street but never mind Jenny because Toby was the one to watch. Pud wanted to wave but wouldn't let himself do it because he couldn't believe an Indian would wave at anyone, not when he was up on his pony watching a yellow-hair come up the canyon.

The yellow-hair stopped about twenty yards down the canyon and picked up a rock, no doubt thinking it was part of Poca's treasure. Poca pulled back his bow and started to kill the yellow-hair then and there with an arrow, but the yellow-hair thought the rock wasn't gold at all and threw it hard at the big wolf that Poca hadn't actually seen but knew was always hanging about. The squaw went on, but the yellow-hair looked up at Poca, and said, "You better get off that mailbox, Pud. Ceil's gonna whip you good, she catches you up there."

Poca was Pud long enough to think it over and decide to risk a minute more.

"What you doing up there?" asked Toby.

Poca glared at the yellow-hair, then swept an arm at the canyon. "Poca's gold!" he said, tight-mouthed.

"Poca's gold?" said Toby, looking confused.

Poca stuck out his chest and folded his arms. "Ugh!" he said, and stared off down the canyon.

Understanding came to Toby's eyes. He offered his bright orange word book to the Indian on the snow-white pony, saying, "I come to trade, red brother. I come in peace. My people call me Buffalo Bill."

Poca unfolded his arms and poked himself with a powerful finger, hurting the knuckles a little. "Poca!" he said, "Pocahaw . . . Poca*hawkis!*" and lifted his chin to the roof of his pride.

"Pocahawkis?" pondered Buffalo Bill. Then a thought too funny to hide in a grin popped out in a sassy laugh. "You mean Pocahontas?" he said, a dance in his voice.

Poca nodded uncertainly, confused by the whiteman's tricky ways.

Buffalo Bill dropped his word book in the dirt and slid down his laugh to a seat beside it. "You can't be *Pocahontas*, crazy!" he said through the cracks in his cackle. "Pocahontas is a *girl!*"

Poca's face got hot with a shame so red nothing but rage could excuse it. "Her *ain't!*" he said, "Her *ain't* a girl!"

"Pud's a girl-Indian, girl-Indian, girl-Indian," Toby babbled, rolling on the ground.

Pud brought his leg over the mailbox and threw himself at Toby. "Her *ain't* a girl!" he cried, and locked his arms around Toby's neck.

The front screen opened and Celia came out on the porch. "Stop it!" she yelled. "Stop that fighting, you hear me! Toby Siler, you get up out of that dirt and get to this house!"

Pud gave one last tug and took his arms from Toby's neck. Toby got up, still laughing, and picked up his word book.

"You get on in here and pull off those school clothes," said Celia. "You heard Mamma tell you this morning you had to wear them today and tomorrow!"

Toby came up the steps to the front porch. "Pud's a girl-Indian, Ceil," he said. "A girl-Indian named Pocahontas!"

Pud dropped himself on the bottom step and started to cry. Toby looked around and down at Pud, the joy falling off his face. "Aww Pud . . ." he said.

Pud started crying so hard it turned his face to the sky and pulled his mouth wide open. Celia went to him and hunkered down so her arms would go around him. She wrapped him like a wall that meant to keep off the hurt, saying, "Now look what you've done you ought to be ashamed of yourself, Toby Siler . . . hush now Pud . . . making him cry his heart out like this after he's been missing you and waiting for you all day like he's done! Come on and hush now, Pud. Here, let's me and you go on in the house and fix us a cracker."

When Toby came from the bedroom in his playing clothes Pud was on the kitchen floor watching Celia take a stack of plates from the cabinet to the round wooden table. Pud gave Toby a glare, then rolled onto his back and started squinting up a ray of sunlight slanting to the floor through a hairpin hole in

51

the green shade on the west window. Toby started toward the table. "Wash your hands first, Toby," said Celia.

Toby turned toward the water bucket on the cabinet, saying, "I am," trying to say it so it would sound like he hadn't forgotten. He washed his hands and dried them on the cup towel, then took the knives and forks and spoons from a drawer in the cabinet. While he unstacked the plates to their proper places on the table and laid the tableware beside them, Celia spread peanut butter on crackers, asking, "What happened today at school, Toby?"

"Me and Billy Dixon run a race at recess and I beat him a hundred miles!" said Toby.

Celia said, "Well, that's nice," and went on spreading the peanut butter on the crackers.

"Then right after rest period Miss Bell read a story 'bout steamboats going all up and down the Missapee River."

"Mis-sis-sip-pi River," said Celia.

"Yeah!" said Toby. "Then she drew a steamboat on the blackboard. Ceil . . . I bet steamboats is awful big, ain't they?"

The talk of steamboats made Pud forget why he wanted to look at the beam of sunlight. He rolled to his stomach and listened close.

Celia finished fixing the crackers and gave two to Toby. She had to lean over to give two to Pud, then straightened up and started eating the one she had left in her hand. Toby put a whole cracker in his mouth and had to work before he could say, "I bet steamboats is bigger than this ol' house . . . maybe big as the cottonmill, almost. I bet steamboats got to have awful big rivers."

Celia's eyes fell on Pud. "Oh Pud!" she said. "You're getting crackers all over the floor!" She watched him until she was satisfied that he was going to pick up every crumb. Then she looked away and Pud stuck them in his mouth.

Jenny came in from the chicken yard carrying the eggs in her skirt. Toby broke for the back door, hollering, "C'mon, Pud!"

Pud got a grip on the cracker he hadn't eaten and bounded to his feet. Celia yelled, "Stop that running in the house!" The screen door flew open and Toby shot out on the porch. Pud made it through before the spring snapped the door back in place again.

Toby got off the porch and took two sticks from under the steps. "Let's play Cowboy," he said, and gave a stick to Pud. Pud aimed it at Toby and said, "Bang!" Toby went limp with disgust and said, "Aww, not yet, crazy!" He thought for a minute, then said, "Playlike . . . playlike you're Billy The Kid and go hide, and I'll be the Sheriff and come looking for you."

Pud had trouble deciding but finally said, "Okay," and crawled under the porch. He crawled out again with a stick about three feet long and stood up and straddled it. "Giddyup horse," he said, and rode off around the corner of the house.

Toby waited long enough for Pud to climb the persimmon tree at the front of the house if that's what he wanted, then rode out after him. He was halfway along the side of the house when he thought it might be a good idea to travel the rest of the pass on foot. Past experience had taught him that The Kid was tricky and mean when you got him cornered. He started for the persimmon tree, but remembered just in time and dropped to his stomach. He started inching forward, silently thankful for that fall and winter he'd spent up in beaver country with the Sioux.

His nose was about three inches from the cutback in the limestone cliff beside the persimmon tree when his sharp ears heard a peculiar sound. He stopped dead still and listened. After a moment a confident smile flickered through his lips and he thought, "That's mighty careless of The Kid, eatin' on crackers with a tracker like me on his trail."

He put his pistol in his left hand so it would be easier to push around the bend in the cliff, but he moved with great care. He knew The Kid's head was just inches away and he meant to get him this time, once and for all. He drew up his legs and got on his knees. He hesitated, motionless, uncertain, then took a slow breath, counted to three in his head, and lunged. As he fell forward he saw the barrel of his pistol come to rest against the forehead of Billy The Kid. He put five bullets in The Kid's skull as fast as he could pull the trigger.

The Kid let out a terrible moan and flopped over on his back. His tongue lolled out the corner of his mouth, all coated with little white flakes of cracker and traces of peanut butter.

The Sheriff got up slow and waited almost a minute before he holstered his pistol. He looked at The Kid with mournful eyes as he brushed the dirt off his stomach and chest. Suddenly the fingers of The Kid's right hand closed on the butt of the pistol at his side. He squinted up at the Sheriff with one pain-filled eye. The pistol swung up. The Kid mumbled, "Still gotta little strength left . . ." and he shot the Sheriff thirteen times.

The Sheriff took out his pistol and threw it on the ground. "You're *always* doin' that!" he shouted. "Every time we play Cowboys I shoot you in the head and right in the heart, but it don't matter. You're everytime saying' you still gotta little strength left and shootin' me after I done killed you and I ain't never gonna play Cowboys with you no more! If you can't even *die* when I shoot in your *brain* I just ain't never gonna play with you no more! CHEATER!"

They were in the persimmon tree at six o'clock when the mill whistle blew. Toby said, "Listen . . ." and Pud closed his eyes and made a face so Toby would know he was listening hard. He stayed that way until the long low drone of the steam whistle ended, then opened his eyes and waited all his patience could stand. "Well?" he said.

"I bet that's how a steamboat sounds," said Toby. "Comin' round a bend in the Missapee River."

"Awww!" Pud snorted. He eased himself to a lower limb and dropped to the grassless circle worn around the base of the tree. His knees gave way and he had to catch his weight on his hands. His eyes went up and didn't blink as he got to his feet and watched Toby hang from his limb for a second or two and drop to the ground. Toby's knees didn't buckle enough to make him use his hands, so Pud's thoughts went back and picked like a skeptical bird at Toby's last remark. He took a deep breath and puffed out his cheeks and went, "Whoooooo!"

Toby laughed, and said, "That's not a steamboat. That's a old owl!"

They went around the house and Pud waited by the steps while Toby went up on the back porch and opened the screen door. He stuck his head in the kitchen, and said, "Me and Pud's goin' to meet Mamma and Papa."

Celia slid the pan of cornbread batter into the oven. "All right," she said, and lifted the lid from the pot of beans to make sure there was juice enough so Papa wouldn't say she had cooked them to death.

Pud followed Toby through the chicken yard,

yelling "Shoo! Shoo!" at the chickens. Toby got the back gate closed and led the way down past the house where Mary Lou Gannaway lived and down the side road to the place where the railroad track cut across to go over the trestle that led to the mill. They stopped at the crossing and looked down the trestle they weren't allowed to cross because they would fall and break a leg.

Men and women with white cotton lint from the looms on their hair and faces came down the tracks, some saying hello as they passed and some going on without speaking, their eyes on the footpath worn in the wood of the crossties.

Toby started waving, saying, "I see 'em! I see 'em first!"

Pud said, "Me! Me!" and waved both arms until he saw them, too. They came across the trestle and Mamma lifted Pud in her arms. "Hello, Darlin'," she said. Papa looked at Toby with his slow grin, saying, "Hello there, big Toby."

After she had hugged him and kissed him enough to make up for a whole day of missing, Mamma let Pud get down. He ran to Papa and hugged his leg while Mamma squeezed Toby's face between her hands and kissed him right on the mouth.

Papa said, "Well now, let's see . . . whose time is it to carry the treasure chest?"

Pud yelled, "Me!"

Toby said, "My time," then remembered what he meant to do because of the crying he'd made Pud do after school.

Pud yelled, "Me! Me! Me!"

Papa looked at Toby to see if he wanted to argue about it. Toby picked up a lump of cinder and threw it down toward the trestle. Papa said, "All right, then. Forever hold your peace." He squatted on his heels there by the railroad track like he did every evening and opened the catch on the black lunch pail. He got the lid open and the jar out of the way, then Toby and Pud stuck their hands in the bottom and rustled through the brown paper until they found what they were after. Papa put the jar back in place and closed the lunch pail, then passed it to Pud.

Mamma took Pud by the hand and Papa took Toby. The four of them came up the side road and past the Gannaway place, Mamma examining the twilight and saying, "The evenings are getting pretty cool . . . I expect you boys will have to start wearing your shoes pretty soon," Papa sniffing the air and saying, "Going to be an early winter," everybody content and home getting closer, the Fig Newtons almost eaten.

School

MISS TRICIA JENNINGS taught the only Second grade at Cottonmill School. Miss Tricia was a woman with a heart. Everyone said so. At recess she'd take Toby by the hand, and say, "Oh Toby, do be careful and don't run so much!" Then Mary Lou Gannaway or Silly Billy or Alato Langley would come right behind in the line and she'd hold one hand so trembly against her rubbery bosom while she reached out so wet and

59

limply the other and "Oh Alato, you've not got a cold again! . . . blessed are the little children . . . here now you *must* take my soft little handkerchief for your tender little nose!"

And that was that.

Hard-Rock Candy

IT WASN'T LONG AFTER Thanksgiving until the getting ready for the Christmas Service at the Methodist Church began. First there was the swing of the Bible from Proverbs to Revelation. From there the rest of it happened almost automatically.

Miss Ruth started the first Sunday in December, giving out parts and rhymes to the two- three- four- five- six- seven- and eight-year-olds in her Sunday-school class. Billy Dixon got to be Joseph in the Nativity scene. Mary Lou Gannaway got to be Virgin

61

Mary. Pud got a rhyme that went

> *Little Fairy Snowflakes*
> *Dancing in the flue*
> *Old Man Santy Claws*
> *What is keeping you?*

Toby got to hold up the pole with the bright star of Jerusalem because nobody else would do it. The others got thought into clusters to sing *Santy Claws Is Coming To Town* or one chorus of *Jingle Bells* because Miss Henrietta's nine- ten- eleven- twelve- thirteen-year-olds were doing *Silent Night*.

Mamma and Celia got to make a red flannel fairy's costume for Pud and a pole-holder's costume for Toby. Papa got to supervise the learning of Pud's rhyme. Jenny got to drive everyone almost crazy trying to make herself able to sing *Away In A Manger* for her solo, an octave too high.

Somehow everything and everyone was ready by Christmas Night, which was Christmas eve. Everyone set out about seven o'clock, coming up all the ways to Luke Street and the warm lights in the windows of Methodist Church shining through the winter dark and the winter cold.

Miss Ruth was grabbing kids as they came through the wooden front doors, getting her cast together. The grownups stood around in their coats feeling *different* than they did in the church house on Sunday or even Prayer Meeting Night.

Down front in the right-hand corner the fat tree that flattened two feet of its top on the ceiling was hung with all the fancy in Cottonmill. There were red ropes and green ropes of bristled paper twisted or sewn on backbones of string. There were bangles and balls, and crayoned and scissored angels, dangling at branchtips. There were pieces of colored glass shaped like lean fangs of ice that hang from eaves, and thousands of long shreds of tinfoil twisting and glittering in the light. Crisscrossing everything, binding it all, were interlocked bracelets of flour-pasted pieces of red and orange and green and all other possible colors of paper.

Here and there and there in the branches were little packages, ribboned and bowed. There and there and here in the branches were cap pistols and dolls. Plain cap pistols, silvery and small, and Buck Jones pistols with pearly-looking handles. Rubber dolls you could drop and not break and dolls with clothes and hair and blinking eyes that could sleep like people.

Under the tree, waiting for Santy Claws to come at the end of the program and give them out, were flat and thick and square packages wrapped in tissue and Christmas paper. And there were long presents that had to be baseball bats, and skates and scooters and even a Red Racer wagon or two. Then there were all the plain brown paper sacks, like the kind at Trager's Store for carrying home groceries. The top was twisted on all of them, but everyone knew they were from the mill and had sometimes an apple and sometimes an orange and always six pecans and a four-inch piece of wiggledy hard-rock candy.

By seven-thirty all the Cottonmill Christians and some that weren't were gathered. The place was filled with Shepherds and snaggled-toothed Angels; Shepherds with Red Goose shoes and rolled-up overalls under their flowing, bed-sheet robes, Shepherds with handles from brooms and handles from mops to make-believe were things you could sit on and twist on and throw and play swords with and poke with and ride like a witch until it was time for them to be Shepherds' staffs. All the Angels had were wings and halos, and the wings felt funny and itched, and the halos slipped. One of the Angels was cross-eyed, another had freckles and a sty on his eye. Another had one wing torn loose from its harness and another had a fat split lip. One Angel nicked a Shepherd's nose with his halo and screamed and cried at the top of his four-year-old lungs when the Shepherd poked him with a staff.

Finally, Brother Cartwright stood up and held up his arms like he knew how to do and settled his half of the problem by saying, "All right, now, if you grown Brothers and Sisters will find a seat, the children have their Christmas program to give us." With that he met Miss Ruth at the piano, and said, "I'll give a prayer, then the rest is up to you."

"Now, Brother Cartwright," she said, "you know

good and well that I'm not able to do all this by myself. Ardell!" she said to the cross-eyed Shepherd, "Leave Bessie's halo alone!"

"But you know I've got to see that the tree doesn't catch on fire," Brother Cartwright said to Miss Ruth.

"I've got it all written down here on this piece of paper," said Miss Ruth. "Just read out what I've got as you come to it so everyone will know what the children are doing." She made him take the paper, then turned to seeing about the music and left him standing there. After a minute he quit looking at the back of her head and glanced down at the paper.

By now all the grownups were more or less settled on the benches. Brother Cartwright said a prayer, saying how grateful everyone was for coming through another year of joys and hardships to another birthday of Jesus the Saviour, and asking blessings on the little children who were about to take part in the program, and on everything. He saw that the Shepherds and Angels were getting restless so he said Amen and cleared his throat while he tried to figure out the instructions Miss Ruth had written on the piece of paper.

"Now why don't we all stand and start things off this evening with the first and last verses of . . . *Oh Little Town of Bethlehem how still we see thee lie . . . above the deep and dreamless* . . . well, I'm sure all of you know it."

Everyone stood, and Brother Cartwright said, "Would you start us off, Miss Ruth?"

Miss Ruth played the part that matches *"the silent stars go by,"* and everyone came in more or less together. Not many sang the last verse because not many knew it. When they got through it Brother Cartwright waited until everyone got settled again, then read, "Now the littlest ones in the Sunbeam Class will sing *Jingle Bells.*"

Half the ones in Miss Ruth's class that didn't have a part in the Nativity came away from the wall beside the piano and lined up bed sheet to bed sheet in the space in front of the pulpit. Miss Ruth had to get up from the piano and straighten it out about who was to stand closest to the Christmas tree. When that was settled she went back to the piano and played the last line of the song, hunching her shoulders and elbows up and down, hoping some of the children would be watching her and get an idea of when to start singing from what she was doing. There was some trouble with *Dashing through the snow in a one-horse open sleigh,* but once they were past that line everything went about as well as she had expected.

It had to be settled all over again from year to year about the clapping, but Brother Cartwright did it when *Jingle Bells* was finished so the rest of them started. The children being clapped at stood there too long or Brother Cartwright read the next thing on the list too soon, one or the other, but everything got all snarled up when the other Sunbeamers tried to start lining up for *Santy Claws Is Coming To Town.* Miss

Ruth was worrying with a sore finger she'd just hurt, thinking about how she should have let the little ones sing *Santy Claws Is Coming* and had the older ones do the one with the hard part about the one-horse open sleigh, so Brother Cartwright came down from the pulpit and two or three of the mothers came from their seats and got the little Sunbeamers out of the way. By the time that was done, Brother Cartwright felt someone might have forgotten what was going to be sung so he read it again before he got back up in the pulpit.

Santy Claws Is Coming sounded fine, even to Miss Ruth and she knew music. Even the Sunbeamers that sang it joined in the clapping, but there's a limit to how long two hundred people can clap at six- and seven- and eight-year-olds, even their own, so it ended, finally, and Brother Cartwright stood up and read, "Next is Pud—I guess I ought to say Alfred, it being Christmas and all—but anyhow he's going to say us a Christmas poem, called *Little Fairy Snowflakes*."

Pud edged out from the wall with the tip of his pointy red fairy cap hanging wrong and tickling his nose, looking all sheepish and uncertain and neckless with his round cheeks and chin scrunched down into his shoulders. His eyes got big when he made it to where he was supposed to stand, and he started looking all around until he spotted Papa and Mamma again sitting on the second bench, right where he knew they

were but had forgotten just for a minute. He looked at
Papa and waited. Papa nodded at him so he blurted,

> *Little Fairy Snowflakes*
> *Dancing in the flue . . .*
> *Old Man Santy Claws,*
> *What is keeping you?*

Then, before the clapping could start, he looked at
Papa again and Papa nodded at him again, so he went
on with the rest of it, just like Papa had taught it to
him, saying,

> *. . . the Vinter Vind,*
> *whi . . . I mean Vistling*
> *Around the corner of the house.*

Everyone knew that last part wasn't in the regular
poem because someone did *Little Fairy Snowflakes*
every year. When they all started laughing with their
clapping, Pud got all excited and not too sure about
things but thinking it must be all right because the
laughing about it sounded good and not *at* him, and
he started laughing too. The ones that could do it
looked away from Pud to where Mamma and Papa
was sitting with Celia. Papa had his arms folded across
his chest, and there was a big grin on his face. Celia
looked like it didn't bother her, but Mamma almost
died.

It took a while for all that to die down, but finally
it was time for the Nativity. Miss Ruth had it worked

out nice. There was hay down front, between the piano and the tree, and there was a manger. Burlap was scattered around and hanging from the rail where you knelt to take Communion. A doll was in the manger, wrapped good, and there was plenty of space around it for standing close. Miss Henrietta's class lined up behind the Communion rail and waited. Toby got to stand in the pulpit and hold up the cane pole with the wire taped to it and the light at the top for the star. The Three Wise Men got in place, and Mary Lou Gannaway came and stood looking into the manger. She was all wrapped in a bed sheet dyed a pale shade of blue.

Jenny went over by the piano and waited while Miss Ruth took the matches she'd brought from home and lit candles and handed them out to the Angels. She got them spread around the way she wanted them, then she lit a big one on a saucer and handed it to Joseph, telling him, "Now, you be careful with that, Billy, and don't set fire to anything." Billy went over and stood by Mary Lou, beside the manger. It was getting pretty crowded but the Shepherds were left to stand where they wanted to and finally everything was ready.

Brother Cartwright went back to the fuse box on the wall just inside the door and waited until Miss Ruth got back to the piano where Jenny was waiting, then he pulled the switch and Miss Ruth played the introduction to *Away In A Manger* and Jenny came in just at the right time, singing it clean and pure and making some of the notes like she was striking glass bells. When she finished there was a hush on the whole place, then Miss Ruth hit three notes, like that, do mi sol, and Miss Henrietta's class came in with the words, singing, *Si-ilent Night . . . Ho-oly Night . . . All is calm . . . All is bright . . .* and it was beautiful. Some of the Angels looked in love with their candles and some of the Shepherds couldn't keep from wiggling their staffs but it was beautiful, all the candles flickering in the Angels' hands and making soft shadows in the hollows and bends of faces and everything, the lights on the tree making dim branch-shadows on the walls and the ceiling, the presents all through and underneath, the star of Bethlehem dipping and bobbing just a little, and the harmony working right in the singing, making you want to do it when the words said, *Sleep in Heavenly Pe-e-eace . . . Slee-eep in Hea-ven-ly Peace.*

When it was over nobody thought about clapping. A few of the mammas got up and started hugging Shepherds and Angels, not knowing exactly why. Mary Lou Gannaway's mamma had tears in her eyes when she hugged Mary Lou. Some of the men cleared their throats and made a point of switching the way they had their legs crossed. All this couldn't have lasted over a minute because it wasn't any more than that between the end of the Nativity and the church house doors banging open for Santy Claws. He came in just when Brother Cartwright turned on the lights, stomp-

70

ing down the aisle with a big sack on his back, saying, "Merrr-ry Christmas! Yo ho ho ho Merrr-ry Christmas!"

The little ones started squealing and the bigger ones started jumping up and down and clapping their hands, yelling, "Santy Claws! Santy Claws! Ohhhh! It's Santy Claws, Mamma, it really is!" and one or two of the biggest ones said, "Heck!" and "Aw shoot! That ain't Santy Claws!" and some that didn't intend to stand for such awful things said, "It is *too* Santy Claws! It is!" and the doubters said, "Crazy, anybody can see it's just Homer Bates," but the faithful replied, "You're the one that's crazy, Crazy! It is too Santy Claws . . . ain't it, Mamma?" and all the time he kept coming down the aisle, saying, "Yo ho ho ho ho . . . it's old Santy! Merrr-ry Christmas! Yo ho ho ho ho!"

By the time he got down by the big tree there were so many kids pushing up around him it took Brother Cartwright's help to find a place to set the sack he swung off his back. "Now you little ones move back a little so Santy can get on with handing out the presents," said the preacher. "Come on now and get back out of Santy's way . . . that's right . . . My my! Isn't it exciting! Get on back, now."

Finally, Santy Claws had enough room for giving. He took a minute looking back and forth between the tree and the sack, making it look like he couldn't decide where to start. Even the ones that were willing to bet fifty thousand dollars to a doughnut hole that it was Homer Bates joined in the yelling for "The sack! The sack you had on your back!"

"What's that?" he said, "What's that you're wanting old Santy to do?" He held his hand to his ear rim and turned his head, pretending to do his best to make out what they were saying. "The sack!" they yelled. "Oh Santy, the sack!"

"Ohh!" he said at last, "You've had all this time to look at the tree and now you want to see what's hid in the sack! Yo ho ho ho!" He opened the sack so his hand would go down its neck in a private way, and pulled out a tiny, shiny red purse and gave it to Emily Gregg for her Ohh and Ahh. His hand went back in the sack and he pulled out a fish-net pocket of marbles. Billy Dixon that once had been Joseph said, "Boy! A whole bag of Zebras!" so Santy gave them to him with a yo and a ho.

It went on like that. There were Yo-yos and tops and bags of marbles, which went to the boys, and there were patent-leathery purses and cards with a rubber ball and jacks and cards with curving yellow butterfly combs and butterfly hairclips, which went to the girls. When everyone had something from the bag, Santy Claws stuffed it under his coat and scratched his neck where the beard was beginning to itch. Then under the Christmas tree he went, making straight for one of the Red Racer wagons. He had some trouble reading the tag, or made it seem like he did, twisting his head from side to side, then his beard got caught on one of the catchy branches of the fir tree. It took some doing but he got it untangled and kept it on his face, then he went at the tag on the wagon's handle again. After a twist and a couple of squints, he said, "It looks like Pud and Toby Siler."

Toby had given it up way back in the middle of *Jingle Bells*. While he was standing paralyzed, taking back the giving-up so the wagon could be his, Pud was under the tree and in the red bed and out and all over it and dragging and butting it out over barricades of presents and brown paper bags. Toby thought, "Pud's," then Papa's voice said, "Toby, you'd better help him."

"You'd better . . . I'd better . . . I . . . mine!" ran through Toby's head, and then he thought, "OURS!" and he flew headlong from the spring of belief to helping and touching and owning.

Finally, except for the decorations, the Christmas tree was clean as a wishbone stripped of wishes. There was nothing left but the brown paper sacks, and a good thing, too, because by then Santy Claws was looking pretty tired. Some of the papas noticed there wasn't much ho anymore in his yo ho, and started helping him see that every kid got his sack from the mill. Before it was through, Brother Cartwright and even Miss Ruth were lending a hand.

When it got down to the sacks that had no takers, Santy Claws stood for a minute with one in each hand, looking around. Then he said, "Well, I guess that's it," to no one in particular, and put them down. After a turn or two he found his big cloth sack and put it across his shoulder. Brother Cartwright said, "Here now, open that sack."

Santy Claws said, "What?" and watched the preacher put two brown paper sacks in the cloth one. "Well, now," said Santy Claws.

The preacher said, "That'll help it carry better."

"I'm much obliged," said Santy Claws, and went up the aisle and out of the Church with one last yo ho ho.

The preacher said, "Well," and the men said, "Well," and Miss Ruth closed the lid on the upright piano. The women said, "Oh, I hate to wake it up," and started inching coats and caps on sleeping Angels. The preacher took a step and said, "Wup!" and steadied himself and said, "Watch out for the marbles."

Widow and spinster and family by family, they went out the doors and left the warm lights in the windows of Methodist Church. They went down Luke Street and down all the ways through the winter dark and the cold, humming hymns or hugging themselves or leading Shepherds or carrying Angels sleeping with hands locked tight on purses and pistols and pieces of melting, wiggledy hard-rock candy.

School

MISS EMILY TURNER taught the only Third grade at Cottonmill School. Miss Emily was "Toby, look at the things I have in this cigar box. No, don't touch them, simply look at them while you can . . . now tell me, what was in the box?"

She'd had a husband who loved her. He'd been dead for seven years and now she was thirty-nine. They'd had one child, a girl, thirteen, first year of High School in Town, a girl, Leaula. They liked each other,

Miss Emily and Leaula, and nothing about it had to be talked between them.

Not long after the Third-grade year began she stopped by his desk and stood there towering and all. "Toby," she said, holding out a book, "I think this arithmetic book will be more fun. It's called 'Mathematics.' Here . . . take it home and work the first lesson whenever you like and think you can. If you think up questions you want to ask, write them on a big sheet of paper and bring them to me. I'll answer them for you if I can."

"Miss Turner," said Toby, taking the book, "what does 'Natics' mean?"

"Matics, Toby, with an M, like Mattress or Music. It means . . . something to do," said Miss Turner.

"Like watching clouds?" asked Toby.

Miss Turner thought for a minute, then said, "No, not that much fun, but almost. And not so useful."

"I don't understand that word very good," said Toby.

"Which one?" said Miss Turner.

"Useful," said Toby. "Is that like jars are for canning peaches?"

"Almost," said Miss Turner. "It's more like peaches are for putting in jars."

"Oh, I see," said Toby. "You turn it around."

"Well," said Miss Turner, "the peaches seem more useful, don't you think?"

"Yessum," said Toby.

"So that makes what?" said Miss Turner. "Clouds are like peaches, and . . ."

"Matics are like jars!" joined Toby.

"Absolutely right," said Miss Turner.

"Why do we have to have jars, Miss Turner?" said Toby.

"Oh," she said, "I can't spend the other children's time on you. Go back to your spelling book. And don't get the other book dirty because I'm giving it to you."

"You mean . . ." said Toby, "you mean I can keep it always and not give it back?"

"Yes," she said. "I mean it," and went to watch the tree Silly Billy was drawing with purple crayon on the lesson page of his speller.

There were all the other things happening at home with Celia and Jenny and Pud, and there was all of Cottonmill, with people and kids and trees and the well and raking the leaves, finally, and frost and winter. But it was packed as tight as can be and as full, right up to Christmas and half-grade time, then suddenly Miss who was really Mrs. Emily Turner had reasons to move away.

Toby couldn't tell who he loved most, Miss who was Mrs. Turner, or Leaula, and both of them were terribly old and leaving and taking away every chance there was for birthdays to let him catch up. He felt about tall Mrs. Turner as he felt about Old Elm Tree where he'd build him a treehouse one day in a high and private place, just as soon as he got big enough to find good heavy boards and hoist them up to the high, private limbs. She was like Old Elm Tree in some ways, strong, and didn't mind waiting. But now she minded, or at least she was going away and that was almost the same as minding. And even if he could bear that, what about Leaula? He felt about laughing Leaula the way he felt about the leaves that made the private for Old Elm Tree's high. She was sunlight on one side and shade on the other, and threads and ropes of sunlight slanting and sliding through the shade, and didn't she know that in four more years he'd be thirteen too and they'd get married if she waited? Oh Leaula, Leaula, Leaula, don't go with her, run away, you can hide in the place up the ladder the place with the big bell at Methodist Church house and I'll send red bean sandwiches and a hairbrush and a piece of mirror up the bell rope! Oh LeAUlaaa . . . what if Mrs. Turner and Mamma and Papa will let us write *letters!*

Apple

PAPA AND MAMMA came in from work on a May evening and there wasn't much talking. Celia had supper on the table so everyone sat down and ate it while it was hot. Mamma asked one or two questions about what sort of day it had been at school, and listened to Pud tell on Toby for running off to Mary Lou Gannaway's house after school instead of playing Cowboy with him, but she didn't do much more than cluck her

79

tongue about any of it so you could tell right away that her heart just wasn't in it.

Close to the end of the meal, Celia and Jenny got into an argument about whose time it was to wash the dishes. Jenny claimed she wasn't supposed to do it because they'd made a deal. She might have got away with it but she got all worked up with really believing it and started saying things about it that everyone knew couldn't be true. Papa finally had all of it he wanted and looked at Mamma to see if she was going to put a stop to it. She must have been awful tired because she didn't even notice that he was looking at her, so he swallowed the last of his coffee to wash down whatever it was he had in his mouth, and said, "All right now, that's enough." Jenny was pretty hurt, believing her side of it the way she did, and might have worked around to saying something about it if Papa hadn't poured himself another cup of coffee and pushed back his chair and went on into the living room before she could think of something.

It wasn't long after that until everyone got through. Before Toby and Pud could run off somewhere Mamma stopped them and made them go out in the garage with her to help sort out the glass jars still fit to use for canning.

By the time the jars got sorted and carried into the house it was getting too dark for much playing. There might have been enough time for a little Hide-and-Seek but Pud stepped on a piece of glass from one of the jars he'd broken and started screaming like he had a dying wound instead of a little cut on the side of his heel that was just barely bleeding. After it got washed and tied up with a clean rag he wouldn't have gone outside and shown that it didn't hurt for at least an hour, even if it had been the middle of the day, so that took care of any Hide-and-Seek.

Celia and Jenny had managed somehow to get the dishes cleaned up and put away, so Mamma decided to go ahead and wash up some of the jars so they'd be ready when she needed them in another week or two. It made sense and all like that, but it meant someone had to carry in three or four buckets of water. One look at Pud was enough to see that he was practically crippled for life in case anything was said about him helping. Toby took the water bucket and went on out to the well without saying anything but thinking plenty.

It took three trips to the well to fill all the pans Mamma put on the kitchen stove. He made one last trip so there'd be water for drinking, then went into the living room and aggravated Pud right up to the edge of what he felt Papa had decided to let him get away with.

In a little bit he heard Celia or someone in the kitchen taking the pans from the stove and pouring the hot water into the washtub. He gave up on Pud and started toward the kitchen door. Something on the shelf under Papa's radio table caught his eye as he went past the chair where Papa sat reading the newspaper. He went on into the kitchen and tried to help put the jars in the washtub but made Celia almost drop one and she said, "Be careful, Toby." Mamma handed him a big piece of clean white rag and said, "You want to sit there at the table and dry them good as we wash them and hand them to you?" He knew by the way she said it that it wasn't a question. He took the rag and pulled the chair around to the right place and sat down in it and waited.

They made the water in the washtub good and soapy and started washing the jars. As they got them clean they dipped them in the pan of hot water that had been saved for rinsing, then passed them on to Toby. The first one he took was so hot it was all he could do to keep from dropping it. He jiggled it around until he got the white rag on it so he could hold it. It had cooled off enough for him to put it on the table with his bare hands by the time he got it dry. He looked down at Mamma and Celia, and even Jenny, and saw them dipping and sloshing their hands in the tub and inside the jars, just like the water wasn't hot at all. It bothered him a lot that they could do that in the water and he couldn't even stand to hold the jars after they got through with them. He tried it again, and again, but finally gave it up and started taking them with the rag wrapped around his hands, hoping nobody would notice. After four or five more jars had been passed and none of them said anything he started thinking about the things that the clean clear glass and the light did to each other as they made patterns on the new checkerboard oilcloth on the table, and wondering how Papa had managed to come home with the apple and put it on the shelf under the radio table without him knowing anything at all about it.

The motion of his hands as he wiped the jar he was forgetting tied in somehow with the slope and the dip of the suds in the washtub on the floor, and there was the rhythm of the women's bare arms sliding down in the water, drowning and saving the jars. All of it caught up his thoughts and let them hover like a butterfly nose-on to the nectar of a rose called apple.

Apples, he knew, came one by one except in far-off cities where all you had to do was line up to get them, but that didn't take anything away from them. Alone or in baskets, each of them huddled sunsets in its cheeks and nights and nights of moonlight in its . . .

"Toby, are you going to dry these jars or not?" asked Mamma.

He flew like the wind to the jar in his hands and twitched it upon the table. His foot rattled the jars collected in a puddle at the mouth of his chair. He picked up the one ringing loudest and rubbed it on its way. Three jars later and calm again, he risked a look at the jar he had rubbed as he dreamed. It stood no taller than the others on the table, but something hummed in the glass itself and hmmm and ohh how it shined.

Pud ran in with a red-crayon-picture to show. Toby gave it a glance and thought it wasn't a very good whatever it was. Pud wanted Mamma to hold it while she looked so he had to wait while her arm combed the water in the tub again for a maybe-somewhere jar. The girls got up off their knees and started taking the dry, clean jars from the kitchen table. Mamma said, "We'd better cap them or they'll be dirty again when we need them." She got up drying her hands on the dish towel she wore for an apron. Pud jumped up and down three times, going, "Unnh!" and flapping his picture. Mamma reached for it, saying, "All right now, Pud, don't get all worked up— Well *my goodness* that *IS* pretty!"

When the jars were closed and put away and the empty pans and the tub were in their places, Mamma and Celia and Jenny went into the bedrooms, looking for something to take to the living room for their hands to do. Toby and Pud went in at once, willing to take a chance on whatever was waiting for them. Toby was chosen by his geography book and Pud stayed snug in the knelling red of his crayon. Mamma and Celia and Jenny came in with snipping and sewing things, and the being a family began.

At last Papa took out his gold pocket watch, round and shiny old. Something he did with his thumb made a thin lid hinge up from the watch's pale flat face. He looked for a minute, then closed the lid on its face and put it away. His left hand moved without him looking to the proper knob on the radio and gave it a clicking turn. By the time his paper was folded the radio had warmed into the news.

Jenny and Celia took their cue from some finger-difference in Mamma's mending and started their crocheting and sewing toward a stopping place. Pud recognized the signs and almost started complaining about having to go to bed, but Papa crossed his legs about then and helped him wait a while longer. Toby went on letting his gaze do as it pleased on a page of his geography book the apple had made impossible to read.

When they stopped the news for the man to tell about Little Liver Pills, Papa looked in his cup and asked if there might be a swallow of coffee still in the pot. Just as he said it, Mamma took the last stitch in the knee of the trousers she'd saved, then put them aside and took his cup as she passed on her way to the kitchen.

Pud couldn't stand any more of it and said, "I hurt my foot and I'm not even sleepy!" When nobody said a word, not even Toby, he knew he had lost again, and started thinking, "When I get big . . ."

The man on the radio said, "So the next time you're feeling down and out with those nagging pains in the back, try Little Liver Pills for quick, smooth, satisfying relief. And now, back to the news." A familiar voice picked it up with, "Today's events in the streets of Madrid seem to indicate . . ."

Mamma came in quietly and handed Papa his coffee, then went to her chair and started looking at the sewing and testing it. Pud left the floor and knuckled his eyes as he came for her lap, protesting a drawn-out, a weary, "Mamma . . ." so she gave it to him. "Shhh," she said, "you can tell me all about it in a minute." He managed a half-hearted groan of displeasure and made a settling upon her so wiggly she had to pull down her dress because it was almost up to her knees.

The news ended, finally. Papa's hand went toward the radio and everybody waited. His fingers found the knob and switched the stranger out of the room. Toby closed his geography book. Jenny managed at last to forget the terrible wrong she'd suffered in the matter of doing the dishes. Pud got so caught up in what was about to happen he elbowed himself through layers and layers of sleepiness to sit up on Mamma's knees. When Papa put the apple in his lap and took his knife from his pocket, even the part of Celia that was still a girl and not a woman slipped through the proud and solemn way she felt about being the oldest.

Papa pinched the apple stem between two left-hand fingers and held it so it wouldn't turn while his right hand turned the apple. Celia, Jenny, and Toby counted the turns in their heads with the ABC's, knowing that the letter that broke the apple stem would be a clue for the name of the one they would marry. Pud didn't know such secret magic as that and counted the turns with blinks of his rounding eyes.

The stem twisted off on E. Toby thought of Emily Rogers and made a face that squeezed his eyes because he didn't like to think it was going to be her. Papa put the loose stem in his mouth and chewed it from tooth to tooth while he shined the apple along his leg just like Toby knew he would. At last the apple gleamed all it could and Papa opened the peeling blade of his knife. He put the sharp tip deep in the dimple the apple had grinned for its stem, then he angled the knife and twisted his wrist and started unwinding the skin.

Pud slipped off Mamma's lap to the floor. The rag that wasn't so white anymore came off his heel but Mamma was the only one that noticed. Her hands picked it up and unpinned it so they could smooth it and spread it against her knees while her eyes went back to tasting the juicy looks on her family's faces as her part of the apple.

Papa stripped the apple with care, feeling a kind of duty to keeping the peel in a single piece. More than that, it seemed somehow to have something to do with not being disappointed with himself, setting a good example. The knife was another of his fingers and ribboned the skin as if unspooling a secret. Halfway down the apple's cheek a shallow brown scar made him frown. He paused to study the scar, and Pud scooted nearer on the floor. The edge Toby felt over Pud because of the almost two years he had on him wasn't enough to let him keep sitting still with Pud that close to Papa. Something he did in his muscles and bones made his chair seem to pour him on the floor and slide him silently across the living-room lino-leum, over its fat roses and lacy green leaves to a spot that would make the edge of age enough again.

The scar of brown on the apple skin frowned Papa into words. "Look here, Kate," he said, deciding to tell the family through Mamma. "You see here where it's healed itself? A bluejay or maybe a mockingbird must'a had this for dessert, just a bite to take the taste of grubworm out of its mouth before going on. A thing like that can set you to wondering, can't it?" He turned then and looked at Mamma, watching her nod as she said, "It does for a fact." After they'd looked at each other a minute and Papa'd gone back to peeling the apple, Mamma studied Celia's look and saw that there wasn't much confusion in it. "She's almost grown," she thought, and smiled at her to let her know there was more to it than the sadness. Celia dropped her eyes to her strong lean hands at rest in her lap. They opened their fingers after a minute and one of them raised to Jenny's shoulder on the sofa beside her. Jenny turned her head but didn't understand the woman's look on Celia's face and put her eyes on the apple again.

By now Papa had it almost naked. The ribbon

was down to the trickiest part. To do it right from now on he had to turn the apple upside-down, but that meant running the risk of tangling and maybe breaking the ribbon. Too, there was the thing about removing the blade and resetting it so the tip could move counterclockwise and go all the way. He looked at the boys and made his face look troubled. "Well, you can see what the problem is," he said. "Do we break it off now and peel out the bottom separate, or take a chance on trying to get it all?"

"Turn it," Pud urged.

"Get it all in one piece!" said Toby.

Jenny copied Celia and Mamma and didn't butt in, knowing some way that it was man's work.

"That's about the way I feel about it," answered Papa. He did all the things he had to do, being careful with the peel, and after an anxious minute he held up the knife with the peel turned down from the tip in one long apple spring.

Pud said, "Ohh . . ." and Toby said, "Boy!" Papa said, "It's kind'a pretty at that." After everyone appreciated it for a minute, Papa said, "Well, how about it, Jenny. You better speak up."

Jenny made a face like eating green persimmons. "Unhh! she said, "I don't see how anyone could want to eat a nasty old apple peel!"

"All right then," said Papa. "Forever hold your peace." He put the stark apple on the folded newspaper across his lap so he could have both hands for slitting the peel down the middle from one end to the other. When it was done and there were two coiling pieces, Toby said, "I don't see how you can do that part and not break it."

"Well, it's not as hard as the other," said Papa, giving one coil to Pud and handing the other to Toby. "All it takes is just a little patience."

Toby and Pud got flat on their backs and dangled the peels down into their teeth. Papa closed the peeling blade and opened the one for slicing. When Celia saw he meant to half it and quarter it she said, "No Papa, just three pieces."

Papa looked up in surprise. "Don't tell me you don't want any?" he said.

"You know how there's times when you crave a thing and times when you don't, Papa," she answered quietly.

Papa studied her, turning the apple in his hand, something like the ball of his life swelling too big in his chest as he looked at the spring just past, seeing the sixteenth birthday she'd had in March and seeing the kind of thing it was, seeing the sixteen years. He looked at Mamma. She didn't so much nod her head as drop her eyelids a little then raise them again. "Well, all right then," he said, looking down at the apple getting brown already where he had handled it. "Forever hold your peace," he said, putting his mind to figuring thirds. Mamma stood from her chair and said, "I'd best go turn back the beds." Celia got up from the sofa smoothing her print skirt and saying, "Yes, I'll come and help you."

When the peel was gone and Jenny and Toby and Pud had eaten the thirds, Papa swirled what was left in his cup around and around to make sure he would get everything, then turned it up and drank coffee grounds and all. He touched his pocket to make sure his knife was back where it was supposed to be, then he put the folded paper under the radio table and used his hands on the ends of the arms to push up out of his chair. He looked down at Toby and Pud and over at Jenny, then back at Pud's face where the pout was building. "Come on now, Pud, and don't start a fuss," he said. "It's time we all got to bed."

"Aww Papa . . ." Pud had to whine once, knowing it was no use.

Papa went across to the front door and turned the key in the lock. On his way to the kitchen, he said, "Make sure you throw those pieces of core in the garbage bucket, and don't leave seeds on your Mamma's . . . and Celia's clean floor." Jenny and Toby made sure they had everything and followed him through the kitchen. Before Pud left the living room, Mamma came in with her long hair down like fire on her pale flannel gown, a clean white rag in her hands for binding Pud's terrible wound in case it got to be something his sleep might need if he happened to remember it.

When all the lights were out Toby lay in the darkness and listened to Mamma and Papa in their bed across the room using slender words to sew scattered, last minute finishing thoughts to the hem of the day. After the last stitch was made and nothing was left but the soft cotton thread of their breathing, he moved his face on the pillow until his nose touched the rim of Pud's ear. "Pud," he whispered, "Pud! I got something to tell you!"

"Leave him alone now, Toby," said Mamma. "He's sound asleep. You can tell him tomorrow."

"Yes, Mamma," Toby answered, moving back to his side of the bed, thinking, "But Jenny and him and me ate Celia's apple and he ought to know." He pulled the cover above his head and wondered why Celia did it.

Pud gave a snort and a twist in his sleep that poked his foot against Toby's leg. "Stay on your own side, Pud," Toby whispered, and pushed Pud's foot with his knee.

"Toby!" said Mamma.

"Yes, Mamma," Toby said meekly, and was very still. After a while he realized that the hard thing against his knee was the safety pin holding the bandage to Pud's heel. He thought about having to bring in all the water for the jars, and then he thought, "He sure is a baby!" He lay there grinning in the dark and grinned his mind all the way to wondering how it would feel to give Pud his part of the apple. A thought and a doze and a wondering later he wondered how it would be to have a whole apple all to himself. Something about it wouldn't let him wonder about it for long, and sailed his mind to a glass jar of light at the core of a whole, dark, pungent apple of sleep.

Domino

GRANDPA AND GRANDMA RAINEY moved to Cottonmill on a weekday, maybe Thusday. It was late in the evening not long before bedtime when a knocking at the front door made Mamma look at Papa and say, "Now, I wonder who that can be this time of night?"

"Sit still," Papa answered. "I'll see." He folded his paper and put it aside, then pushed up out of his chair and went to the door. As he opened it, someone on the front porch said, "Well, they're alive, at least," and there they were.

Papa said, "Why, look who's here . . . it's your Mamma and Papa, Kate."

Mamma put her sewing aside in a hurry, saying, "Oh, my goodness!" as she stood from the deep, fat sofa. Granny started through the door, hung like a halltree with clothes and bundles and small cardboard boxes tied with string. Papa's hands moved out and he said, "Here, let me take some of that."

"No, thank you, I can manage," Grandma replied. She paused in the doorway and said back over her shoulder, "Mind now, Coper, and don't bang that crate on the door."

"Go on, Old Woman," said Grandpa, and followed her through the door with a trunky thing hugged in his powerful arms. He put it down and took off his cap. One thick, square hand lifted to his bare head and tried to mash some order on his black, bushy, unmashable hair.

Grandma stood there, all piano wires and thin cables on her small spring and stainless steel frame, with a look on her face that made you know she wouldn't shed a parcel until something she had in her mind was spoken and settled. One look at her was all it took to know she would live for a hundred years. Mamma circled around her, trying to find openings somewhere so she could hug her. Grandpa looked at Papa with his fierce black eyes intent as caves beneath their briery brows. His coarse ears pulled back the corners of his mouth in a stained, square-toothed grin, and he said, "Pleased to see you, Siler."

"Pleased to see you, Coper," said Papa, and they made a brief handshake that left them without a good place for their hands. As they started rolling cigarettes, Grandma said, "I've got to have my say."

Papa's eyes went up to examine her face, and he said, "All right." Mamma made herself stand still, and said, "Why, yes, Mamma, what is it?"

Grandma went on, her voice flat with determination. "We're finished with the Home Place. It's gone. We've come here to live."

"Well, both of you know you're welcome here," said Papa. "Now let's put your things somewhere."

"Let me finish," said Grandma.

"Old Woman . . ." said Grandpa.

Papa nodded at her, and said, "Go ahead."

"Just a night or two," said Grandma, "until we find a place of our own. And there's work to find."

Papa said, "I'll ask at the mill, but things . . ."

"I don't know machines," said Grandpa.

"Oh, there'll be something," said Mamma.

Grandma studied her face, then Papa's, then said, "Coper, take off your coat," and started unloading herself.

There was gathering and putting out of the way, and getting coffee and settling for talk.

"Where's the younguns?" asked Grandma.

"All sound asleep," Mamma replied.

"Well, now . . ." said Papa, smiling at Grandpa, and settled back in his chair.

Mamma said, "Mamma, what happened? You said the old Home Place was gone?"

Grandma said, "Yes. Burned to the ground." Mamma's face began getting ready for a moan. Maybe to stop it, Grandma said, "It's just as well."

Mamma groaned anyhow. "Ohhh," she said, "and this you brought is all you saved?"

"All that matters," Grandma replied.

Grandpa's hands went *phugg* on his blocky knees as his bottom lip pushed up the top one, and he said, "The sonofabitch went up like a haystack in August."

"Coper," said Grandma.

"Old Woman, let me be," Grandpa replied.

"But surely you got out your pretty butterfly quilts and things?" asked Mamma.

"We didn't," Grandma said evenly.

"And what about the clothes and things . . . that shawl you wore at your wedding?" asked Mamma.

"I told you," said Grandma, an edge in her voice. "Burned. Everything burned."

"Any idea how it started?" Papa asked Grandpa.

Grandpa pursed his lips and thought about it for a minute, then said, "Heat lightning, maybe."

"Well, that beats all I ever heard," said Mamma, shaking her head.

They were quiet for a while as they thought about

it, then Mamma got tears in her eyes. She felt around for a handkerchief and finally took a clean rag from her wicker sewing basket and blew her nose. She looked at the rag in her hands, then folded and wadded it and took a deep breath, and said, again, "That beats all I ever heard."

They moved into the Shipley place, across the road from Samuel Pepys' Elementary School. There was no steady work for the first few months, but carpentering now and sewing then and always pecans to shell for the Monarch Pecan and Candy Company in Town made it so it wasn't bad. Then Herschel Thornhill got fired for passing out one day in the coalhouse, and Grandpa got the janitor job across the road at the school.

It was handy for Grandpa, and Grandma, too, them living just across the road from Grandpa's work. The schoolhouse was a square, two-story brick building that sat behind a row of cottonwood trees. It had four rooms downstairs and four rooms up. Each room downstairs was a grade: First, Second, Third, Fourth. Three of the rooms upstairs worked the same. Fifth, Sixth, and Seventh, and the other one was a place for assembly and P.T.A., with a piano and a stage. The grade-rooms had coal-burning potbellied stoves, and blackboards across the back that slid up into the walls. Behind the blackboards a space two feet deep was for hanging coats and putting lunches and making kids stand in the dark when they got too noisy or wouldn't mind the teachers, who acted like they didn't know that the one being punished back there with the blackboards down was busy going through all the lunchbags and eating anything that had the taste of sugar.

Maybe there were a hundred students in all. But living just across the road, Grandpa could go before daylight to the smaller red brick building that sat at one side of the school and get the buckets of coal from the middle part between the toilet at one end for the girls and the one for the boys at the other. By the time he'd have enough coal carried in and a good fire going in each of the potbellied stoves, Grandma would have breakfast waiting on the table. And during the day, when he swept down the halls with oily-smelling saw-dust and caught up on everything else, like mopping the toilets with pine-tar water, he could go across the street to the house and have a good strong cup of cof-fee while he sat with his mind at ease and listened to Grandma tell all about how they were going to manage to buy the cow or the hog or whatever it was.

It was handy for Mamma and Papa, too, Grandpa and Grandma living where they did. With Celia and Jenny getting grown and in Town every day at the High School, it worked out nice in the way of a hot mid-day meal for Toby and Pud, and someone who cared to keep an eye on them and see that they didn't get hurt or something between the time school let out and the mill shut down in the evening.

Because of the way it felt and not because of planning and thinking, it got to be part of living for Grandma and Grandpa to come to the Siler's for Sunday dinner, after Sunday School and Church. Grandma would bring a pot of chicken and dumplings, or maybe a spice cake or apple pie that was good but not as tasty as Mamma's. Papa always got a kick out of the way Grandpa and Toby would be impatient for dinner to be over and out of the way.

Mamma and Grandma would talk about Brother Cartwright's Sunday sermon while they worked with Jenny and Celia, getting things hot and finished and on the table.

As soon as Grandpa ate the last bite of whatever dessert might be, he'd drop his fork and push back from the table, saying, "All right, Siler, you've stalled long enough, let's go get on with the slaughter."

Papa would chew a few more times, then swallow the bite in his mouth. He'd look up at Grandpa and grin as he said, "Why, Coper, surely you don't mean that!"

"Mean it?" Grandpa would say. "Mean it? Get up from there and you'll see!"

"Ahhh, Coper," Papa would reply, shaking his head as if he was terribly sad. "You're a glutton for punishment. Don't you know by now . . . haven't you learned in all this time that you just can't beat me?"

And Grandpa would stand with his fists on his hips, short and stocky, legs spread, looking earnest and determined as rock, a ponderous scowl on his face all dressed up in a fearfully harmless glare. Their eyes would put hammerlocks on each other, then Papa would sigh and break away, saying, "All right, then, if that's what it takes to convince you. Go set up the table, Toby."

It was Toby's pleasure to get the light folding table from its place behind the open front-bedroom door, then take it into the living room and set it up for the lesson, for that's what their domino games were to him; a school where he learned things he couldn't say but knew were going to be useful. The gloss in the middle of the black, stiff paperboard top of the table was worn and dull from shuffling, and that was part of it, somehow. The shuffling of the bone dominos and the taking them unknown for a hand made him almost think of something, but he didn't know what it was or how it worked or when he would need it; all he knew was a feeling he had that it just might come in handy. It was the same with the rest of it, only just a little bit clearer. Like the counting with marks, which Papa did because Grandpa didn't know how to read or write or count, except in his head in some way he had made for himself that wasn't like two plus two. But the marks; one was five and two in a cross was ten. A row of five crosses and five rows of crosses was game. You could count five or ten or fifteen or twenty or on up to no telling how many, but to do it you had to make all the ends of the pattern add up to a certain number. To make fifteen, for instance, you had to have something like six and four and five. It couldn't be sixteen or fourteen, it had to be right on the money to count. And the playing had to be done in a certain way. Four dots had to be joined with four dots. You couldn't join a four-dot with a three-dot because it wouldn't work and wasn't right and would ruin everything.

Even with his strange way of doing it, Grandpa was pretty good at figures, but it didn't make any difference because Papa was good at eyes and faces. After Grandpa played once or twice, it seemed that Papa could tell what he had and knew just how he would play it. And Grandpa would shake his head and say, "Well, Jonah swallowed a whale!"

At the end of eight or ten games, Grandpa would open the cuffs of his shirt and push his sleeves up above his elbows, then fold his heavy, hairy arms across his chest, and say, "I swear, I never in all my life met a man to beat you for luck!" At that point Toby knew that Grandpa would win the next few games, and he thought about that, and studied Papa's face for signs.

After Christmas that winter, in February, lots of ice and even a little snow on the ground, it must have been the time for it because Toby got the mumps. It looked like a cold and a sore throat at first, but morning came and he had no neck, just jaws straight down to his shoulders. Mamma and Papa talked about it, deciding he had to be moved to Grandma's and Grandpa's house so Grandma could tend him while he was sick. They didn't like the idea of having to move him, not with the mumps, but it couldn't be helped.

They bundled him good and Papa carried him. Mamma stayed close as they walked, tucking the blankets around him and cautioning Papa not to jiggle him any more than he had to. Grandma took charge when they got to her house, supervising the settling of him in the spare bed room in the room just off her kitchen, a room with lots of windows where the sun could get in if it made up its mind to shine.

Mamma said, "Darlin', don't be getting out of bed, now, and keep yourself covered up, does it hurt? Oh, I wish I didn't have to go to work so I could look after you . . . Celia will come after school this evening and read to you if you feel like it, won't you, Celia . . . now Pud, don't you and Jenny aggravate him . . . Mamma, don't you think it's better he's got them on both sides at once?"

Mamma and Papa went on to the mill. Later, Celia and Jenny went to catch the interurban they rode to Town and High School. Pud left at last, crossing the road to the schoolhouse, where Grandpa was having some trouble with the Third-grade stove.

Up in the morning, Grandpa came in for a rest and some coffee, but Grandma sent him down to the store and all over Cottonmill, looking for a head of a hog. It ended up with him having to go in to Town before he found one. Grandma put it in a pot and hammered its jawbone so she could scrape out all the marrow. Maybe she put something secret in with the marrow, but when it was ready she spread it all over Toby's neck and wrapped it with a piece of flannel. It smelled and felt kind of funny but Toby didn't feel like saying anything and knew it wouldn't do any good if he did.

Grandpa was in once or twice, then Pud came in from school and leaned on the bed and looked at him for a while, going "Goop! Goop!" because he looked a little like a frog. Then Grandma gave Pud a piece of sausage inside a cold biscuit and he said, "Toby looks like a frog," and he put on his coat and ran out to play.

Jenny and Celia came in from High School and Celia offered to read but Toby said, "I don't care," so she didn't. Jenny said, "Oh, I hope I don't catch them . . . Grandma, can you have them twice?" Celia said, "Well, we'd better get Pud and go on home and fix supper."

It was a little out of the way but Mamma and Papa came by on their way home from work. Papa said, "Just take it easy, son, you'll be all right." Mamma fussed with his cover, and said. "I'll come back after while and stay till bedtime." Grandma said, "Now Katherine, there's no need for you to come out again in the dark and cold. I expect I know how to take care of him."

"Why Mamma, I'm not the least bit worried about

that," said Mamma. "I just need to be with my kids when they're sick, that's all."

After Papa and Mamma left, Grandma made Toby sip some hot broth from a cup. Then Mamma came back with some custard she'd made, and she fed him part of that and washed his face and gave him an aspirin and billed him and cooed him and loved him to sleep.

By the next afternoon Toby felt good enough to be interested in the sunlight, the motes that rode it, the heat it made, even through the windowpane, and the way it fired the tiny, silken hair on the back of his hand. When Celia came he closed his eyes and was quiet but imagined everything that was and that happened in the story she read.

Papa came with Mama that night after supper. He could tell they were pleased with the way he felt by the way they made jokes about the size of his neck. Mamma said, "We'll bring your school books when we come by in the morning. You don't want to fall behind in your figuring and studying." As they got up to leave, Grandpa couldn't resist saying something to Papa about dominos. "Siler," he said, "watch out on Sunday. I've figured a few surprises."

"Why, Coper," Papa grinned, "you know you don't stand a chance."

"Uh-huh, well, we'll see about that," said Grandpa. "Still, if I had some of your luck in drawing the hands . . ."

"No luck to it," said Papa. "I pull them face down from the shuffle, the same as you. It's how you play what you get that counts."

"Siler, you trying to tell me the kind of hand you draw don't make a difference?" said Grandpa.

"No," said Papa. "All I'm saying is you're stuck with whatever domino you draw and you've got to play it, so you try to play it the best way you can and don't let it play you."

"Tobias," said Mamma, "I'd like to see that Pud has a bath tonight."

"Mamma, can I take this rag off my neck?" said Toby.

"Humph!" said Grandma.

"Now, Toby, you leave that poultice right where your Grandma put it," Mamma replied.

"But Mamma . . ." said Toby.

"Now, Toby . . ." said Mamma.

"All the same," said Grandpa, "you best be ready. I'm giving you fair warning."

"Well," said Papa, "you never can tell . . ."

Around ten o'clock the following morning, the front door opened and someone came into the house. Toby's mind jumped all the way from Egypt. He listened long enough to make sure it was Grandpa, then went back to the pyramids in his geography book.

"Old Woman," said Grandpa, "the coal was heavy this morning."

"I'll pour you some coffee," said Grandma.

"No, not now," Grandpa answered. "I think I'll lay down and rest for a minute."

"All right, Coper," Grandma replied, and went on with her chores in the kitchen. Five or ten minutes passed, and then she remembered something she wanted to mention. She came through the room where Toby was having his mumps and straightened his covers, saying, "Keep those feet and legs covered up, you hear."

"Yes, Ma'am," said Toby.

She went on into the other bedroom, then Toby heard her say, "Coper, we've got to figure a way to . . . Coper, what's wrong . . . Coper? Oh God, have mercy!"

The way she said it made Toby put down his geography book. "Grandma?" he called, "Grandma?"

"Oh God have mercy!" she cried.

He jumped out of bed and ran into the room. She was there on her knees beside the bed, and Grandpa was still and silent across it. "Grandma!" Toby cried, and his eyes started streaming.

She pulled herself up on the bed and on Grandpa. Her hands and arms and her shoulders and back looked little and skinny and brittle in her clothes. One look at her was all it took to know she would never live for a hundred years. Toby ran to the mill in a pinwheel quilt and his underwear.

At home in his own bed two days later when Mamma and Papa came home with Grandma and

Brother Cartwright and other men and women from the funeral, Toby heard the women and Grandma telling each other, "He had a good life." When the preacher and the others were gone and no one was left but the family, Toby called for Papa.

He came through the door and stood beside the bed. "Yes, son, what is it?" he asked, his face and his voice quiet and gentle.

"Why did Grandpa have to die?" asked Toby.

"Well," said Papa, seeming to go into himself as he sat on the edge of the bed, "it's one of the dominos."

Revival

MISS RUTH HAD ON a white organdy dress with something pale blue underneath that was like a slip, except it had shoulders. Just as Miss Ruth came in, Ma Haskins started down the aisle, passing out the song books. Everybody waited until Ma said, "Evenin', Sister Burkes," and some of them let their heads make stiff nods, and said, "How do, Miss Ruth."

Miss Ruth worked in the mill, the same as all the rest of them, and knew everybody there that evening, kids and all. She nodded back at everyone that spoke, but didn't smile and kept moving on up the aisle with a serious look on her face. That was all right. Everybody knew she was like that when she was wondering about the songs.

When she got up front, Brother Cartwright walked down the two steps from the pulpit and shook her hand. Charley Haskins giggled right out loud. Charley was Ma Haskins' boy. He was about thirty or forty years old, but he giggled at most anything he wanted to because he was crazy. Besides, seeing a man shake hands with a woman did look funny, even if the man was a preacher.

Brother Cartwright opened his song book to where he had it marked with a slip of paper. Miss Ruth stood there with her arms folded and sort of resting on her big stomach while the preacher turned the slip of paper over to get to the writing he'd done on it, and after a minute he said, "I thought it would be good to start off with *Are You Washed In The Blood* . . . right after the congregation gets settled good, see, and let that lead in to the opening prayer." He raised his eyes and looked at Miss Ruth and she made him wait a minute while she thought it over. When she finally nodded her head, the preacher looked back down at his notes, and said, "And then, right after the prayer, I thought it might be good to sing *There Is A Fountain Filled With Blood.* Down there in the chorus, where you get to ". . . *wash all my sins away*——" you see how that ties in with the first one?"

While all this was going on, Ma Haskins finished passing out the song books and got Charley away from the bell rope and made him sit beside her, right up front. He didn't mind that, because Toby Siler and six or eight other boys and girls, all about ten or eleven years old, were sitting on the front bench, too. There were only twenty-eight benches in the whole church, but they were all pretty full. Each side of the church had five tall windows. All of them were raised as high as they would go. But it was still hot, being July like it was. A lot of the women swished at themselves with fans made out of shell-shaped pieces of cardboard stapled to short wooden handles. Most of the fans had "Ranger's Funeral Home" printed across them, but some of them had "Garrett's Snuff."

Brother Cartwright got Miss Ruth's okay on *There Is A Fountain Filled With Blood*, then asked what she thought about starting to play *Softly And Tenderly Jesus Is Calling*, just as he started with the invitation. She couldn't argue with that, and went on over to the piano and sat on the bench with her hands folded in her lap. Brother Cartwright got back in the pulpit and everybody quieted down, hoping he wouldn't want them to stand up and sing the first song, but he got his arms all spread out and raised them up, so everybody got up. Then he said, "Let's all turn to page a hundred and four in our hymnals, and start the meeting this evening by singing that fine old hymn, *Are You Washed In The Blood Of The Lamb?"*

Miss Ruth made some great big chords for an introduction, and pretty soon everybody was singing so loud it was all you could do to hear the preacher.

Right as the song ended Charley Haskins started giggling, but Ma got him settled down before he could get too excited, and then Brother Cartwright gave a fine opening prayer, giving thanks for all the good things that had happened so far during the revival, like having eight new ones join the church, and seventeen rededicate. Then he asked a blessing on all the sick and needing, and on poor old Charley Haskins, and wound up by making a special plea for guidance on that last night of the revival, so his words might inspire all those who were almost persuaded to go ahead and take the big step to everlasting life. It came to about ten Amens, all told, so Brother Cartwright figured he was getting off to a good start. He let everybody sit down and sing the second number.

Everything went along pretty good until about halfway through the sermon when Oscar Dixon had to stand up so his wife could get past and take the baby outside and let him nurse. That must have been what he wanted, all right, because she no sooner got outside with him than he stopped crying. She came back inside with him in a little bit and he went to sleep and didn't make another sound all during the rest of the sermon.

Over close to the end you could tell Miss Ruth was any minute going to start playing real soft, just by listening to the change in Brother Cartwright's voice. And then she did start playing, and Brother Cartwright started talking fast, like he was in a hurry to get everybody to singing before Charley started giggling or the Dixon baby woke up and started crying again, or something like that happened. He got everybody to stand up again and worked in the page number, and pretty soon everybody was singing *Softly and ten-der-ly Je-sus is calling, call-ing for you and for me* . . . , saying the words low and making them sound like they was coming to their mouths from some place solemn and far away.

After the first stanza everyone kind of hesitated and started picking out different ones and looking at them, but the preacher started right in on the second stanza, so everybody followed along.

About halfway through the second stanza it began to look like nobody was going to go down front, then all of a sudden Mary Lou Gannaway turned around and picked up her little pink purse off the bench behind her, right there where she had been sitting all evening between the Simpkins boy and Toby, and she walked right up there to the preacher and stood stiff and quiet while he got down on his knees and hugged her and started whispering to her. Everybody else kept right on singing.

Brother Cartwright stopped the singing at the end

of that stanza. He whispered to Mary Lou a little more, then he stood up and laid his hand on her head, and said, "Little Mary Lou has come, seeking forgiveness for her sins and asking to be admitted to this church so she can give her life for Jesus." Then he looked down at her and kept his hand on top of her head, and he said, "Mary Lou, darling, I know Jesus loves you just as much as you love him, and is awful proud to see you standing here, declaring your love right out in the open so anybody that wants to can see it."

Mary Lou stood stiff and still for a few more seconds, and then it looked like all the starch seemed to go right out of her, and she laid her head against Brother Cartwright's hip, and her long curls started dancing up and down about half an inch every time her shoulders trembled.

Over in front of the bench where she had picked up her purse, Toby stood staring at the back of Mary Lou's head, watching the light make different patterns on her hair when it jiggled up and down. A strange feeling came up in his chest, a feeling like nothing he'd ever felt before, and then the preacher asked everybody to close their eyes and start singing at the beginning of the song again.

Even with the singing going, Toby kept his eyes open, looking at the light on Mary Lou's hair. Just loud enough so you could hear him, Brother Cartwright started asking, "Won't you come? Won't you come tonight? Won't you come down and stand here tonight before Christ with Mary Lou?" And everybody dropped their voice down, softer and softer, and sang . . . *come home . . . . come home . . . ye who are weary come ho-o-ome. Softly and ten-der-ly Je-sus is calling . . .* , and before he knew he was going to, Toby started crying. He felt the big wet tears drip down his face, and tasted the salty taste, and suddenly he realized that Ma Haskins was the one standing beside him, one arm around his shoulders, dabbing at his wet face with a tiny handkerchief that smelled all at the same time like lavender toilet water and Vick's salve, whispering to him in her wrinkled voice, "Don't you love him, Toby? Don't you love the baby Jesus?" and the people singing *calling for you and for me . . .* , singing it real soft and sad, and the preacher saying, "Won't you come?"

Toby turned around and looked at his Mamma, standing behind him between the second and third benches, and he saw that she was crying, too, and looking at him like there was some awful ache inside her. He couldn't make his throat work the first time, but he swallowed hard and managed to ask, "What must I do, Mamma?" before his throat stopped up again.

For a minute it looked like the ache got bigger in her eyes, and then she said, "You do what *you* want to do, Darlin'." Toby kept looking at her, but that's all she would say. In a little bit he turned around and looked back at Mary Lou and saw that her hair wasn't jiggling as bad as it was before. The preacher said,

"Won't you come?" and Miss Ruth played softer and prettier than she'd ever played before, and everybody just barely whispered, *Come home . . . come home . . . Ye who are weary come ho-o-ome*, and Toby walked out from under Ma Haskins' arm and up to the preacher and reached down and took hold of Mary Lou's hand, just before Brother Cartwright's hand came to rest on top of his head.

Folksong

AWE WAS INVOLVED in the way Toby's fingertips closed on the poised crisp locust skin he found clinging to the bark of the tree he was climbing. The awe put feathery down in his fingertip gentleness with the brittle used-to-be skin. To touch such a thing and to look at it, too, was to wonder how *anything* could do such a trick. And to wonder such things on the swaying limb of a tree in a good afternoon was to peer through an unleafed window of tree and consider the slow, great flexing of a cloud.

From another tree a pair of scissor-tails jumped straight at the sky to stitch a tight circle above the tree peak, like women crocheting, guttering pleasantries at each other for as long as it took to fall again into the green arena of their privacy.

On a persimmon branch three feet from Toby's eyes a lizard hid in its skin as it slid along, then stopped abruptly. The quick shrink and swell of its throat and blink of its eyes made Toby wonder why lizards always look so surprised.

The coarse laugh of a crow came pesting from the brush beyond the trestle, or somewhere, and the fat heat of midafternoon dozed contentedly in the leaves of the trees.

The hobo sun leaned its light against the westward stare of things while shadows up to no good slipped off to the east using every hiding place to weave their dirty trick of night.

White leghorn hens started clucking themselves from the thick skirt of honeysuckle hanging long from the hips of the well. They batted their eyes in disbelief while they dusted the sleep and the dirt from themselves, then strutted and staggered their way to a drink from the puddled end of the pipe that ran from Mamma's new sink in the kitchen.

A wiry sound slurred its way to Toby's ears as the

back screen door stretched its spring as it opened. After a pause just long enough for a pair of pretty good eyes to check all the backyard places a boy of eleven might be, a carrying voice said, "Toby?" saying it in a where-are-you tone.

Toby didn't answer but unwrapped himself from the limb he was on and dropped to the ground around the persimmon tree.

"To-beee!" Mamma called again, her tone saying answer me now.

"Yessum, I'm coming!" he answered, and the warm grass whispered itself to the soles of his feet as he ran. He came down the side and around the back corner and slid to a stop by the bottom step of the porch. Mamma's hands were halfway to her mouth and cupped in the way they had to be for letting her make the belled velvet call of a dove, a thing she said she'd learned when she was a girl. Seeing her hands like that made him wish he had stalled a little longer, long enough for the sound he liked so much to come at least once through her thumbs and the cup of her palms.

From there his thoughts made a loop that let him say, "I saw a robin while ago, right there in the 'sim-mon tree, and while I was in it!"

"Well I declare!" she said, her hand trying to smooth down his cowlick while she looked him over. "Don't seem to be many robins around anymore. What's that you got in your hand?"

"Aww," he replied, opening the cradle of his hand, "just an old locus' skin."

"Ummm," she said, "Well, get the bucket out of the kitchen and draw me some water now. Your Papa'll be coming home before long. And fill up that tub and get yourself cleaned up."

"Yessum," he replied. As he moved up the steps to the porch her hand fell away from his head and the cowlick hung across his forehead as before.

The well was a special place. The cool and the smell of the rope when it was wet, the glistening trails that snails made across the wooden door on the top, and the smell of honeysuckle hanging around it all were things he knew and liked on hot summer days. They seemed to be involved somehow with the taste of the cold clear water.

When the tub on the back porch was full he pulled up one more bucket, looping the rope on the peg, then closed the door in the cover and took the water into the kitchen.

A pry and a press of a thumb and a finger unfastened a shoulder strap. He looked out across the porch and the chicken yard to make sure there was no-one about, then he dipped the other shoulder and the overalls dropped down his legs and around his feet. He stepped into the washtub and the cold water took his breath away.

From somewhere the other side of the door to the

kitchen, Mamma said, "You expect to get clean without using soap?"

"I forgot," he replied.

He heard her make a clucking sound. Not much later the door hinges squeaked and the spring closed the screen with a snap. He looked back over his shoulder and took the soap and washcloth from her hand.

"There," she said, "I swear I don't know how those chickens keep getting out of their pen—You want me to scrub your back?"

"No ma'am," he said, sinking down in the washtub. "I can do it," he added, and started a healthy lather across his shoulders.

She went back in the house, a knowing smile about to break loose at the corners of her mouth. She came back one more time to bring clean overalls and a towel but didn't say anything and went back in to get supper started.

Papa came in from work and found things waiting just right on the table. Toby ate three pork chops and played around with his snap green beans, then gulped half a glass of iced tea, and said, "That sure is a good smellin' apple pie, Mamma!"

Mamma gave him a smile, but said, "Now none of your tricks, young mister. You can wait for us. Here, why don't you eat some more of this gravy? I believe I put too much baking powders in these biscuits . . .

aren't you going to finish those good green beans? I swear, you don't eat enough here lately to keep a cricket alive!"

"Aw Mamma," said Papa, "why don't you let him go ahead and eat his pie."

"Now Tobias," said Mamma, "how is he ever going to learn any manners till you stop doing that?"

"Oh, I don't know so much about that," said Papa. "It seems to me there's not much wrong with their manners, in spite of all my interferin'. And besides all that there's not enough good apple pie in this world . . . a man oughtn't be kept away from it when it's handy."

"Well I'll tell you one thing," said Mamma, cutting the pie, "it's not on my head if Jenny and Pud have disgraced us these past two weeks at their Aunt Rena's with Mamma.—What do you suppose made Mamma decide to stay down there with Rena instead of coming on back on the bus tomorrow when Celia brings back the children?"

"Now Kate," said Papa. "there's no point in going into that all over again. It's like I told you last night before you went to the bus depot with Celia . . . with Coper gone, maybe she wants to roam around a little, nothing more to it than that. Well, I guess I can stand a piece of that apple pie for myself about now."

"That crust looks all right, doesn't it?" asked Mamma. "Son, does it taste all right to you?"

Toby swallowed part of the last bite of pie in his

mouth, and said, "It's awful good, it really is . . . can I have another piece?"

"Yes," said Mamma, "if you'll wait till I serve this one to your Papa. And don't try to talk with your mouth so full."

" 'Scuse me," said Toby, then traded a grin with Papa about the way Mamma tried to hide it when you pleased her.

Papa got his pie and took a bite. "Ummm!" he said, nodding.

"I guess I'll try a bite or two myself," said Mamma.

Papa swallowed once or twice, then said, "What you been up to today, Toby?"

"Not anything," said Toby, taking the piece of pie Mamma passed him on a saucer. "Just playing."

"Did you clean out the droppings in the hen house?" asked Papa.

"Yessir," said Toby, "I did that this morning, early, and took 'em over to Mr. Cuna'ham's. He said to tell you he sure did thank you."

"Mercy sakes!" said Mamma. "Can't you two talk about that when we get through eating?"

" 'Scuse us, Mamma," said Papa, "we wasn't thinking, was we, Toby? You know, you're getting' to be a consid'able help to us, Toby. Your Mamma's been telling me all you've done these past weeks while she's been off work with her back. I reckon you'll be a man full grown before long."

"I'm going to chop all them 'simmon sprouts in back of the garage tomorrow!" said Toby.

"He's gettin' so big he don't want his Mamma scrubbin' his back no more," said Mamma, giving her face the grin she had saved.

Toby got red in the face and dropped his eyes to the flakes of pie crust on his saucer. His racing thoughts found something at last, and he said, "I saw a robin in the front 'simmon tree today."

After the supper dishes were dried and put away, Toby got out his dictionary and read what it said about locusts and lizards and turned to a place that had a picture he'd seen as he thumbed through for locust. When llama was read about too he put the book back in place and went out in the front yard to look at the sky. The sun was gone but the bellies of clouds were still shading into violet. "It's almost time," he thought, and went back in the house. He went straight through to the back bedroom and took the old domino table from under the bed he shared with Pud. Besides the wear of the domino playing the table showed signs of the kites he pasted and the clocks he tore open and the studying he did on spiders and moths and butterflies and all the other things he could find that caught his fancy in his roamings through the roads and gullies and fields around Cottonmill.

Along the back edge of the folded table was a black rectangular case. He put it on the bed and worked the catches near each end. When the case was open he reached into the blue velvet cradle and took out the silver clarinet Mr. Cunningham gave him early that summer.

On his way through the house he took the ligature off the hard rubber mouthpiece and put the reed in his mouth to get it ready. He left the house with a "Watch out for snakes" from Mamma. He crossed the yard and headed down Luke Street toward the small clump of willows in the open field two hundred twenty-odd yards away. By the time he got there the reed was out of his mouth and under the ligature on the mouthpiece, ready for use.

He tried to move quiet as he parted the patchy screen of willows and crept to the edge of the small shallow puddle of a pool. He sat on the bank at the spot where he sat every night. He made himself be still, and started the waiting. The color was gone from the sky and the willows were starting to disappear.

At last the moment came when everything was silent and still, the moment the world changed gears. Then it seemed like the whispery humming that came to his straining ears was the endless sigh of the whirling earth as it curled its circle like a top spun by the sun . . .

and night began.

"Keeraaawks!" the bold bass downbeat was sounded by the old boss frog, and the evening's starlight symphony began.

"Qooreeek!" replied the oboe toad.

A cricket clocked its "Chitit!"
"Keeraaawks!" the bass.
"Qooreeek!" the oboe.
"Chitit!" went the cricket.
"Keeraaawks!"
"Qooreek!"
"Keeraaawks!"
"Qooreek!"
"Chitit! Chitit! Chitit!"

The beat was made, and now the altos, the French horn frogs, the choruses of crickets, the tenor frogs, all sang their counterpoint.

"Keeraaawks!"
            "Engh!"
"Qooreeek!"
            "Unngh!"
"Keeraaawks!"
            "Engh!"
      "Chit!"
    "Ungh!"
"Chitit!"

Toby put the mouthpiece of the clarinet in his mouth and started counting in his mind, "One thousand, two thousand, three thousand, four thousand, five thousand, six thousand, seven . . ." until he was certain the beat was the same as last night, the night before, last week . . . the pulse never varied.

The tips of his fingers closed all the keys and he

played a low note, soft, to a count of four, then held his breath and listened with his fear.

"Keeraaawks!" boomed the bass.

"Engh!"

"Qooreeek!"

"Unngh!"

"Chitit!"

"Chitit!"

The symphony continued, and Toby cried. He had come each night for a month, studying the song, fathoming the beat. For a month he had tried to play with them, a month of one note that stunned them or startled them to silence, but their silence was shorter each night until now . . .

He had to be sure. He blew the long, low note again, and the symphony continued as before. He tried another note, and then another, and the symphony continued as before.

"I've done it!" his mind rejoiced. "They're used to me now! They think I'm a crazy new kind of frog with a difference in its head. Or maybe they know . . . but I don't care! They're letting me play! They're letting me play!"

And he sat lost and alone, playing himself a companion, spellbound with the sound of his loneliness. The moon came up like a desperate wish and gave the willows their looking-glass pool.

"Keeraaawks!" grumped the bass of the old boss

frog and ker-plunked a ribbon the willows might wear as he leaped into the water. Toby cocked an ear, and the night was still. It came again, tolling softly, the call of the dove. He stood from the bank and slipped through the night-dreaming willows, his gaze on the yellow squares standing watch in the night.

The dove call came once more and he raised the clarinet to his mouth. He played the three-note tune of the call. A shadow moved in the doorway square of yellow, and he grinned and jigged and blew the silver call of the dove to the moon until he was home.

Black-Eyed Peas

IT STARTED OUT with the stillness balanced on the pale brink of daylight like the other summer days in Cotton-mill. Everybody got up and dressed as the day stacked up in their heads. Toby and Pud went out and saw the kitchen light come on in the Gannaway house while they scattered grain to the quiet chickens. Papa got the first hot water off the stove and had his middle of the week shave at the cabinet while Mamma and Celia and Jenny made breakfast around him.

When the biscuits and bacon and eggs and butter and gravy were gone, Mamma got up from the table saying, "Celia, you'll have to fix us a lunch and send it by Toby, I guess."

Celia said, "All right, Mamma."

"It's all done but putting it in the stove and letting it cook," said Mamma. "No, now, Pud, you'll have to stay here with Celia."

"Aww Mamma . . ." said Pud and Mamma put her hand on his neck, already thinking about something else.

Mamma and Papa left when the second whistle blew. After the water was drawn and brought in from the well, Toby and Pud built a dam at the side of the house where the pipe drained the water from the kitchen sink. They made roads and bridges all around it using scraps of kindling wood for road graders. After that they climbed the persimmon tree and got over on the roof up under the branches and wrestled until Celia heard them and came out threatening to whip them if they didn't come on down. She made Toby come in the house and wait while she took the hot meat loaf out of the oven and got the lunch box ready. Pud was waiting for him when he came out the back-door screen. He grabbed him from behind and almost got a hammerlock on him before he got away.

He went out through the chicken yard and down the path to the side road and along the road to the railroad track, the mill pushing what he was going to do to Pud out of his mind. It was too big, for one thing, big and old and roaring, men and women going inside it in pairs early in the morning, saying hello to others, all of them going to their places on the first or second or third or fourth floor, fitting into their jobs like keys in some big clock, part of the roar until nearly dark and coming out tired and slow with a layer of cotton lint on their hair and faces like mold.

He came across the trestle and stopped at the bottom of the broad steps below the entrance, looking in to the stairs. He scuffed his feet around in the cinders scattered there at the steps so the workers wouldn't track mud inside when it rained. While his feet got black he took his gaze out of the entrance and looked around to see if anyone was coming up the railroad track or standing in one of the windows up above, watching him stall around. Nothing stopped his gaze and it went on up to the clouds coming slow and high across the top of the Mill. His feet started moving him around the side of the steps and against the white wall, his head going back more and more until he was staring straight up the side, his face against it, the clouds moving and the wall tilting and swaying and about to fall over on him and crush him under a mountain of white-painted brick. He shut his eyes and didn't open them any more than he had to until he was away from the wall and up the steps.

It was all right once he got inside. Up in the weave shop on the second floor where Mamma was a weaver and Papa fixed looms there were wheels and axles and pulleys and belts running everywhere. There was the main belt coming right up out of the floor, turning a wheel big around as a tank car. Over there was the axle that hung from the ceiling, one end of the weave shop to the other, pulleys all spinning and whining and belts going this way and that. The electric lights were burning like always and pipes up near the ceiling were spraying the mist that kept the threads from breaking and made rainbows all around the lights. Some of the boys he knew waved at him or grinned when he went past where they were taking the spools of thread out of the bag they carried them in and putting them in the boxes on the looms, doing it because they were big enough and because it was all the same, all part of it, no different than Jake Owens getting drunk on Saturday night, no different than death coming and the women going with covered dishes and sympathy and Grandma Jackson sitting up all night with the corpse, no different than Ma Haskins getting re-saved every time a new preacher came for a special revival at Cottonmill Methodist Church and making them take her out to Mistletoe Lake again and dip her under because she didn't hold with sprinkling, all the same, all taken for granted, no different than rain.

Mamma's face brightened when she saw him coming through the looms trying to act grown up and serious and not let on how embarrassed he was, her not proud because he was bringing the lunch box or trying to act grown but just because he was alive.

When he got to her looms she gave him a quick hug and hollered something in his ear, knowing he wasn't used to it and wouldn't hear anything over the noise of all the belts and pulleys and axles and looms, then she had to go on because one or another of her eighteen looms was going to go on stopping every two or three minutes when the spool ran out in the shuttle.

Papa came up from some place and said something too but didn't hug him, knowing how it might make him feel with everybody giving him every look they could spare. He took the lunch box and mentioned Toby to follow him on over by the back windows to his work bench. He put the lunch box on the bench and fished around in his overall pockets until he came out with one of the bullet-shaped spindles that came on both ends of the wooden shuttles. He gave it to Toby and got him trying to spin it on the metal top of the work bench when Ben Gilstrap walked up, foreman of the weave shop and a friend, born and raised in Cottonmill and a steady hand at the mill for close to twenty-five years, older than Papa and two dollars a week more on his paycheck but not the kind to ever put on any airs about it. He couldn't seem to talk without putting his hand on the listener's shoulder or touching him someplace, but that was all right because everybody knew him and knew it was just the way he was.

Toby quit trying to spin the metal spindle and Ben Gilstrap started acting like he didn't stop by the house three or four times a week in the evenings to talk over this and that with Papa. He took Toby and Papa by the arm and pulled them against the windows so Toby would be sure to hear, squeezing his arm and saying, "Why, who is this, Tobias? Just feel of that arm. Why, this can't be your boy, can it? He's about a man grown, I tell you that for the gospel truth!" Then he dropped his hands and went on off toward the far end of the weave shop to see about something.

Papa tried one more time to show Toby how to make the spindle work, then took out his Sears Roebuck pocketknife and made Toby understand he'd better run on because there was work to do. On his way out, Toby stopped by Mamma's looms for a second and she hugged him good-bye.

About the middle of the afternoon there was a good hard shower that cooled things off for a while and all the kids up and down the street ran out and got their clothes all wet wading in the ditches. Then the sun come out hot as ever and Celia made Toby draw water out of the well in the back yard and pour it in the washtub. When the tub was full she made him and Pud get in and take a bath while she fussed about their clothes getting full of red clay out of the ditch and promised to skin them alive if they got even a speck of dirt on their clean clothes before Mamma and Papa came in from work. A few of the neighbor kids came around later on and a game of Soldiers and Indians got started. Then, when Pud hadn't been massacred but nine times and right in the middle of Custer's Last Stand, the mill whistle blew and Toby and Pud took out lickety-split to wait down by the railroad tracks.

After supper Clyde Dixon's boy Eddy came by with his hair slicked down and walked Celia and Jenny but mostly Celia over to the church house for choir practice. Toby and Pud played in the yard for a while, then Mamma made them go draw a bucket of water and wash their feet for bed. Papa dragged out the rocker and sat on the porch with Toby and Pud while Mamma sat in the rocker and shelled dried black-eyed peas in her apron. Pud was all wore out from running and whooping and getting massacred and right after he got his feet washed and things quieted down he flopped over on the porch and went to sleep.

Mamma and Papa started to talk back and forth, mostly for Toby's benefit, hinting all around it without coming right out and saying anything that let on if they remembered or not about the next day being Toby's birthday. While they were aggravating him this way Ben Gilstrap come up and Mamma got quiet so the men could talk and went on with shelling her black-eyed peas. Toby sat there quiet as Mamma, rubbing his toe back and forth on a rough knot or something he'd found in one of the floor planks of the porch. In a little bit Ben Gilstrap pulled out his tobacco and rolled himself a smoke. Nobody said anything until he got it lit up, then he said he guessed it was safe for him to be getting back home as his woman Bertha ought to have the buttermilk about churned by now. While he was chuckling at himself his eyes dropped over on Toby sitting there hunkered in the twilight worrying the knot with his big toe. His arm reached out just as his jaws started to working and he started squeezing Toby's arm and shoulder while he said, "I swear, I never seen a boy shoot up the way this'n a yours has done these past months, Tobias!"

In a joking kind of voice, Papa said, "Aw, Ben, he ain't much more than a runt if you get a good look at him in clear daylight, ain't that right Kate?"

Mamma went on shelling her black-eyed peas and answered calm like such a thing was too far-fetched to argue about, "He's a fine and healthy boy."

"I tell you what, I'll leave it up to you, Ben," said Papa. "You'd never know to look at him he's going to be ten years old when he gets up in the morning, now would you?"

"Ten years old?" Ben answered, saying it like he was dumbfounded. "Is that a fact? And tomorrow you say? Well, I never would a thought it! But I guess I got to go along with Kate if you don't mind, Tobias. I swear, this shoulder feels ever bit as powerful as yours or mine." He dug his thumb down in Toby's shoulder like he was proving it, then he said, "I guess you'll be ready to tote that fillin' an' bring in that bacon money, won't you Toby, now that you're near grown. Course with school startin' in next week and all, I expect we won't get the good a that strong pair a shoulders but after school and on Saturday. Still, you bein' such a promisin' hand I guess I'll have to let you tote for your Ma. Wouldn't seem right to put you anywheres else, Toby. Wouldn't seem fair to you."

Toby bent his head down harder and didn't say anything. Ben Gilstrap acted kind of surprised and took a drag on his cigarette that would have burned his fingers except for the calluses. He held the butt where he could look at the fire between his thumb and finger for a minute, then let it fall by the steps and ground it in the dirt with his foot while he said, "I expect you'll be mighty proud to be up there a'totin' for your Ma . . . won't you?"

Toby felt everybody looking at where he was sitting. He squirmed around for a minute, hoping somebody would say something but they just waited like they were awful curious to know what could all of a sudden be going through his head. He kept waiting, wishing he'd fell over and gone to sleep when Pud did, wishing he could run off someplace and hide. Finally he knew he wasn't going to get out of saying something so he mumbled, "I druther not do it, Papa."

"Speak up now, Toby," said Papa.

Toby started scooting over closer to where Mamma was sitting quiet and still in the rocker. He turned his head up, trying to see her face in the dark. Just when he knew Papa was about to say something else he started talking all in a rush, "It wants me, Papa, I heard you say it! I heard you say out here on the porch one evenin' how it was after ever'body and 'specially Pud and me . . . didn't he, Mamma? Didn't he say it meant to swaller ever'body? Didn't he? And it's fixin' to fall, and wants to swaller me, and you're not goin' to make me go and let it swaller me, are you Papa? Papa? And it's always leanin' out over me, and big, and . . . don't let Papa make me go and let it swaller me, Mamma. Please! Please! Please!"

Mamma came out of the rocker letting black-eyed peas scatter any way they wanted to, kneeling and putting her arms around him and holding him tight and him squeezing her with all his might and crying like his heart had broke, her hugging him and holding his head tight against her bosom and saying, "No sir! You hear me! No sir! Nothin' or nobody on God's green earth goin' to put my baby in that mill, not an' him feelin' this strong about it! No sir! No sir, you hear me! Not in a million years!"

Pud woke up and saw the dark and heard Toby crying and the sound of his Mamma's voice, and he started crying too. By now Papa had stood up to go comfort Mamma and Toby, but went over and swung Pud up in his arms, talking to him soft and moving over by Mamma and Toby.

Ben Gilstrap just stood there, not knowing what to say or what to do, just stood there shuffling his feet and trying to figure it out. Toby kept saying it was going to swallow him and Pud kept crying, thinking it was bound to swallow him too, whatever it was, and finally Ben Gilstrap made a gravelly kind of noise clearing his throat and said, "I guess I best be gettin' on back. I expect Bertha is wondering . . . ever'thin' all right, ain't it Tobias? I didn't mean . . . what is it, Tobias? I just can't figure what . . ."

"Put your mind at rest Ben," said Papa. "Every-thin's going to be all right here in a little bit. Kids are just . . . now hush, Toby . . . Pud . . . lots to do in this world and life besides workin' in that mill. Hush now. Everythin's all right . . ."

"Well, I . . . good night Tobias, 'night Kate. See you in the mornin'," said Ben.

Papa answered, " 'Night, Ben."

Ben Gilstrap went on home. In a little while Mamma and Papa got them quiet. Toby got a lamp out of the house and helped Mamma gather up most of the black-eyed peas off the front porch. Celia and Jenny got back from choir practice, then they all went to bed.

Old Elm Tree

OLD ELM TREE WAS TALL was old was a world, a world so private it didn't have to hide. It gained its privacy in the looks it made for every looker's eye. On its thick trunk-wick it burned like a great green flame. For twenty yards around it the ground was emerald cool and somehow diamond dry but damp on the hottest summer days.

Old Elm Tree was selfish with its secrets. Its hide was tough and its leaves were fat and thick over all

its secrets and continents and seas and cuddled rooms.
Spiders and lizards and suns and moons and seasons
and life and death itself were Old Elm Tree's secrets.
Old Elm Tree was a layered meat of years. Tall and
tawdry as live elm can get, it had stood full grown for
maybe a hundred and who knows how many years. It
seemed a place where you might want to build a treehouse, or so Toby's muscles told him.

He was glad to know they were ready at last, his
muscles. He'd been waiting for them for what seemed
to him a hundred thousand years. They'd worked well
enough for the climbing and exploring of the last
years, but the boards he had spotted and hid were always too heavy to hoist into place, until now. Maybe
the climbing he'd had to do in picking the highest the
safest the very best place for the treehouse had pulled
his muscles day by day and climb by climb to the
strength of now, but no matter how or what, or even
why, they were ready for building, and so was he.

One by one from the weeds that hid them down
by the railroad siding he carried the usable boards of
the abandoned boxcar door. One by one through the
kite-stick weeds in the trestled gully that handled the
hard spring rains he carried the heavy boards to the
mouth of shadow closed on the moisture around Old
Elm Tree's greedy roots. That took a day.

The day it took was something Toby knew was a
piece of him, for lately he had begun to learn important things about time. Something about the way peo-

ple look and talk did part of it. Papa had a way of narrowing his eyes as he gauged the fading light of the day. "Night's coming," he'd say. "We'd better get finished with this." And in the late hours untying her apron as she came from the kitchen, Mamma liked to say, "I'll swear I don't know where this day has gone to!" He'd paid no attention to any of that, but attention didn't matter. He heard it as it happened and the hearing stayed in his head; slipped into it like a sky slips into a tree. The hearing and staying of what he heard made a knowing that didn't need saying. Nights *come*. Days *go*. It seemed he had known it forever.

Anxiously early next morning he sneaked away from Celia's concern and Pud's innocence. On his way to Old Elm Tree he saw that the sky was blank with blue and the early sunlight lemoning its way to the brass it would be by ten-thirty. Going down the road past Mary Lou Gannaway's house the rusty dust puffed cool up through his toes. At the railroad track the rail he walked was cold with chill conspired in the night. He left the rail at the trestle and slipped down into and through Kite-stick Gully, his eyes on a spot two-thirds up Old Elm Tree where the treehouse would be before the day was gone.

The creosote heavy weatherproof boards were where they had to be. With that off his mind he took one final look around for the sake of privacy and set to work. From his waist and under his shirt—Celia might have noticed it—he unwound the baling wire and the forty-foot rope he'd made from pieces of clothesline and stout hemp string and anything else that would work. He tied one end of his rope on a fist-size rock. The rock went into the back pocket of his pants and he started up the tree. It wasn't easy at first but that was one of the reasons why he and Old Elm Tree were friends. Its lowest limbs were a good twelve feet up off the ground. Its trunk was too fat for even a grownup to hug around, but there were knots and cracks in the leathery bark like warts and wrinkles on an old woman's neck and he knew where they were and which ones to use.

He reached the first spread of limbs and from there the going was easy. In no time at all he was straddling one of the building limbs where the tree-house was going to be starting right now. It was a room; the tree itself had built its roof and walls with thicknesses of other limbs and branches of leaves. It was high, the room, at the peak of his courage, and a blind act of faith beyond. It had secret windows, windows that started inside as small as the pupil of an eye then flared out like tunnels like funnels like green bells of horns that could drench the whole world with a music of gazes. All it required was a floor, and the tree had even grown a foundation for that. Two strong limbs just right for the boards forked straight out from the trunk.

He nodded yes to himself and took the rock from his back pocket. When the rope he had trailed was pulled up the tree he crawled out the limb he was straddling and tied the free end around it. When that was done he put the end with the rock up over a higher limb that would work as a pulley. The rock dropped down through the branches, taking the rope back to the ground. It was tricky and scarey and dangerous scooting back on the limb but he made it to the trunk of the tree and in no time at all was back on the ground with the rope and the rock.

He tied on the first board and climbed Old Elm Tree again. The strong but skinny and knotty rope worked well enough but was sort of rough on the hands. By the time the first board was up he was glad he hadn't tried it with two like he started to do. He got it untied and across the two limbs before he realized that the baling wire he needed was down there on the ground where he'd dropped it to get at the rope. He said "Awww!" at himself, then decided he had to go down anyhow to tie the next board so it didn't matter. He dropped the rock-tailed rope through the tree and started the trip himself. By the time he reached the ground he had forgotten to be unhappy with himself about the wire.

He decided his waist would be the best place for carrying the wire and still have his two hands free. He wrapped it around himself before he tied the rope on the second board and climbed the tree again.

He bent the baling wire back and forth. The working broke the wire and he passed it over the board and around the limb and pulled it tight. When it was through he wanted to crawl the board itself to the other limb where the other end had to be wired down. It felt all right when he jiggled it, but he scooted back on the limb he was on and crawled out the other one because he was just a little bit too afraid.

It felt good having both ends fastened and board number one in place. He let himself admire what he had done. After a minute he thought of the railroad rail. The board looked three times as wide, and was. "I bet I can stand up and walk it!" he told himself, but then looked down and thought, "It's awful high . . ." He crawled across the board on his stomach, a little upset with himself, then pulled the second board up through Old Elm Tree. Four of the ten boards later he almost beat the dinner mill whistle home.

There were questions from Celia, and that brought questions from Mamma. After a bit, even Papa got interested, maybe because of the way Pud complained. Jenny was too caught up in something of her own to become involved. Or maybe sympathized, none of which—questions or fancy or sympathy—helped Toby at all with Papa's interest, which any minute could turn into a judgment. "Toby," said Papa, "what have you done with all that time?"

Toby thought hard. He knew he had to, for if his answer wasn't right from start to finish he knew he might as well forget his dream of a ship in a sunlighted always-yellow sea. He decided the only thing Papa might let by would be the truth, and not even that if he didn't agree with all the things it was and meant. "I'm building something, Papa . . ." He frowned and looked down, twisting and fidgeting with the effort it took to think of what to say. "Something awful important."

"Oh?" said Papa, his interest seeming to stay about the same.

"Yes, yessir," Toby managed.

Papa waited, which meant everyone else did too. Knowing there was no way out, Toby blurted, "It's something I've *got* to have!"

Papa just took his gaze off the biscuit he was buttering and looked Toby in the eye, holding it there just long enough to say, "Is that why you want it . . . because you got to have it?" then looking back at the juicy biscuit and watching it all the way till his fingers popped it into his mouth.

For some reason *that* didn't seem at all hard to answer. "Yessir!" Toby said in a hurry, "I couldn't want it so bad unless it was something I've *got* to have!"

"Un-hnnn," said Papa, chewing. Another biscuit and a rinse of coffee later, Papa gave just a glance of his eyes that had nothing Toby might use. "You going to get hurt?" he said.

"Nossir, nossir!" Toby replied, then added, "I . . . I don't think so."

"You better find out," said Papa, not even glancing.

"Nossir, I won't get hurt, no sir!" said Toby.

"Well then . . . ," said Papa, "are you making any trouble?"

"Nossir, not any at all," said Toby, knowing he'd reached the last hurdle. Papa let him know he had cleared it by saying, "Are you going to get finished with it?"

"Yessir," said Toby, "I'll finish the making today."

"All right then," said Papa, and went on eating.

Mamma began, "Tobias, don't you think . . ."

"I'll need him for water if the washing gets done this afternoon," said Celia.

"I'm not going to have anyone doing anything with me!" said Pud.

Papa answered all three by saying, "It can wait. He's got him a bone to chew."

Toby thought, "He's going to let me do it!" and before the joy of that wore off it made him think, "Didn't even ask me what," and finally, "He's going to *trust* me!" and that was a strange and sobering thing because it meant if things went wrong there'd be absolutely nobody else to blame for any of it and as even Papa would say plain hell to pay! He thought about that until dinner was gone and Mamma and Papa gone back to work and the dishes scraped and stacked and

Celia said, not unkindly, "You think you're grown now, don't you?"

It was tricky getting away from Pud not in spite but because of what Papa had said. It made Pud have to try to follow him. That took fast running out of the way before it was safe to get back to Old Elm Tree out of breath and wringing-wet with sweat. Since he had to wait anyhow to make sure it had worked and Pud wouldn't find him, he rested. The one o'clock under the big trees if anywhere breeze had him almost dry by the time he took his back from Old Elm Tree's trunk but leaving his damp backprint and tied the next board on the rope hanging down.

He didn't notice, particularly, but learned a new thing on each of the six trips he made up the tree with the other boards that afternoon. With board number five he learned about a thing half finished. It came as he wired the second end of the board in place and took a good look at what was done so far and realizing there was at least that much still left to do before he could say about it, "It's done." He learned that a thing half finished is at least three things; a certain place; maybe even the middle middle of a certain chunk of time; and a certain way of measuring things with eyes and hands and bones and life itself.

With board number six he learned about not getting hurt or making trouble because you said you wouldn't.

With board number seven he learned about the

thing he did when he said he wouldn't and wondered what its name might be.

With board number eight he learned how nice it feels when you know for sure that you can do whatever you said you would or wouldn't.

With board number nine he learned that the nice is a handy thing to have when you're tired.

With board number ten he learned about board number ten.

He was tired that night when he went home from his work a little before Mamma and Papa came home from theirs. It was a different tired than any he'd known in his twelve almost thirteen quick years, a deep tired, a whole tired, a worn out good night's sleep tired, but when he woke up the next morning he woke to a ship for it, and a sea of it, and an all summer long and a world, and maybe even a lifetime. . . .